the

theory

of

light

and

matter

winner of the flannery o'connor award for short fiction

the theory of light

& matter

ANDREW PORTER

the
university
of georgia
press
athens
and
london

Published by the University of Georgia Press
Athens, Georgia 30602
www.ugapress.org
© 2008 by Andrew Porter
All rights reserved
Designed by Mindy Basinger Hill
Set in 10/15.25 pt Electra LT Standard
Printed and bound by Thomson-Shore
The paper in this book meets the guidelines for
permanence and durability of the Committee on
Production Guidelines for Book Longevity of the
Council on Library Resources.

Printed in the United States of America
12 11 10 09 08 C 5 4 3 2 1

Library of Congress Cataloging-in-Publication Data
Porter, Andrew, 1972–
The theory of light and matter / Andrew Porter.
        p.   cm. — (Flannery O'Connor Award for Short Fiction)
ISBN-13: 978-0-8203-3209-3 (hardcover : alk. paper)
ISBN-10: 0-8203-3209-7 (hardcover : alk. paper)
1. Children—Fiction. 2. Teenagers—Fiction.
3. Responsibility—Fiction. 4. Ethics—Fiction. I. Title.
PS3616.O75 T47 2008
813'.6—dc22   2008023989

British Library Cataloging-in-Publication Data available

"Coyotes" © 2003 by the Antioch Review, Inc. First appeared
in the *Antioch Review* 61, no. 1. Reprinted by permission of
the editors.

"The Theory of Light and Matter" reprinted from *Prairie
Schooner* 80, no. 2 (Summer 2006) by permission of the
University of Nebraska Press. © 2006 by the University of
Nebraska Press.

"Connecticut" © 2005 by the Antioch Review, Inc. First appeared in the *Antioch Review* 63, no. 1. Reprinted by permission of the editors.

contents

acknowledgments

I WOULD LIKE TO gratefully acknowledge the following publications in which the stories in this collection first appeared, some in slightly different form: "Hole" in *Story, Story Competition Winners* (F&W Publications), and *Art at Our Doorstep: San Antonio Writers and Artists* (Trinity University Press); "Coyotes" in *Antioch Review*; "Azul" in *One Story*; "The Theory of Light and Matter" in *Prairie Schooner*; "River Dog" in *Epoch*; "Departure" in *Ontario Review* and *The Pushcart Prize XXXII: Best of the Small Presses* 2008 (W. W. Norton/Pushcart Press); "Merkin" in *Threepenny Review*; "Storms" in *StoryQuarterly*; "Skin" in *Other Voices*; and "Connecticut" in *Antioch Review*.

These stories could not have been written without the generous support of the University of Iowa Writers' Workshop, the James

Michener/Copernicus Society of America, the W. K. Rose Foundation and Vassar College, the Helene Wurlitzer Foundation, the Sewanee Writers' Conference, and Trinity University.

I would also like to thank the many teachers and friends who have helped me out with these stories along the way: David Louie and Frank Bergon at Vassar for their invaluable early encouragement and for their continual support and friendship over the years; Marilynne Robinson, Frank Conroy, James Alan McPherson, and Barry Hannah at Iowa, and later, Richard Bausch at Sewanee, for their infinite wisdom and kindness; my dear friends, who have read these stories in many forms and who have helped me out in more ways than they realize: Jonathan Blum, Amber Dermont, Holiday Reinhorn, Seth Hurwitz, Cyndi Williams, Dan Gluibizzi, Sashi Moorman, Melissa Sorongon, Mike Fallon, David Levinson, and Adam Scott; my wonderful colleagues in the English Department at Trinity University; Hannah Tinti and Maribeth Batcha at One Story; the nice folks at Iowa (especially Connie Brothers); Michael Knight at the Helene Wurlitzer Foundation; and of course Erika Stevens, John McLeod, Dorine Preston, Courtney Denney, Stacey Sharer, and the rest of the incredible staff at the University of Georgia Press.

Finally, my deepest gratitude to the amazing Jenny Rowe, who has read these stories in so many incarnations she probably knows them better than I do at this point and whose unwavering support and patience over the years has been the main reason I was able to write them in the first place; and of course, most of all, to my family, to Mike and Di, and to my mother and father, who first instilled in me a love of reading. This book is for you.

the

theory

of

light

and

matter

hole

THE HOLE WAS AT THE END of Tal Walker's driveway. It's paved over now. But twelve summers ago Tal climbed into it and never came up again.

Weeks afterward, my mother would hug me for no reason, pulling me tight against her each time I left the house and later, at night, before I went to bed, she'd run her fingers through the bristles of my crew cut and lean close to me, whispering my name.

Tal was ten when this happened, and I was eleven. The backs of our yards touched through a row of forsythia bushes, and we had been neighbors and best friends since my parents had moved to Virginia three years before. We rode the bus together, sat next to each other in school, even slept at each other's houses, except in the summer when we slept out in the plywood fort we'd built under the Chinese elm in Tal's backyard.

Tal liked having the hole on his property. It was something no one else in the neighborhood had and he liked to talk about it when we camped out in the fort. The opening was a manhole that Tal's dad had illegally pried open, and it led to an abandoned sewer underneath their driveway. Rather than collecting their grass clippings and weeds in plastic bags as everyone else on the street did, the Walkers would lift the steel lid and dump theirs into the hole. It seemed like a secret, something illicit. We never actually knew what was in there. It was just a large empty space, so murky you could not see the bottom. Sometimes Tal would try to convince me that a family of lizard creatures lived there, just like the ones he swore he'd seen late at night by the swamp—six-foot-tall lizard people that could live on just about anything, twigs or grass, and had special vision that enabled them to see in the dark.

That was twelve years ago. My family no longer lives in Virginia and Tal is no longer alive. But this is what I tell my girlfriend when I wake at night and imagine Tal talking to me again:

It is mid-July, twelve summers ago, and Tal is yelling to me over the roar of the lawn mower less than an hour before his death. His mouth is moving but I can't hear him. Tal is ten years old and should not be mowing the lawn, but there he is. His parents are away for the day on a fishing trip at Eagle Lake, and Kyle, his older brother, has offered him fifty cents to finish the backyard for him. Tal and I are at the age when responsibility is an attractive thing, and Kyle has been nice enough on a few occasions to let us try out the mower, the same way my father has let us sit on his lap and drive his truck.

It's drought season in Virginia. No rain in two weeks and the temperature is in triple digits, predicted to top out at 105 by evening. The late afternoon air is gauzy, so thick you can feel yourself moving through it and when I squint, I can actually see the heat rising in ripples above the macadam driveway.

Tal is hurrying to finish, struggling through the shaggy grass, taking the old rusted mower in long sweeping ovals around the yard. The back of his T-shirt is soaked with sweat, and from time to time a cloud of dust billows behind him as he runs over an anthill or mud wasps' nest. It is the last hour of his life, but he doesn't know that. He is smiling. The mower chokes and spits and sometimes stalls and Tal kicks at it with his bare feet. In the shade of the Walkers' back porch, I am listening to the Top 40 countdown on the radio, already wearing my bathing suit, waiting for Tal to empty the final bag of clippings into the hole so we can go swimming at the Bradshaws' pool.

The Bradshaws are the last of the rich families in our neighborhood. Their children have all grown up and moved away, and this summer they are letting Tal and me use their pool two or three times a week. They don't mind that we curse and make a lot of noise or that we come over in just our underwear sometimes. They stay in their large, air-conditioned house, glancing out the windows from time to time to wave. We swim there naked all the time and they never know.

It's strange. Even now, I sometimes picture Tal at the end of the driveway just after he has let the mowing bag slip into the hole. He is crying and this time I tell him not to worry about it.

"Let it slide," I say. "Who cares?"

And sometimes he listens to me and we start walking down the street to the Bradshaws'. But when we reach their house, he is gone. And when I turn I realize he has started back toward the hole and it is too late.

In the retelling, the story always changes. Sometimes it's the heat of the driveway on Tal's bare feet that causes him to let the bag slip. Other times it's anxiousness—he is already thinking how the icy water is going to feel on his skin as he cannonballs off the Bradshaws' diving board. But even now, twelve years later, I am not sure about these things. And I am not sure why the bag becomes so important to him at that moment.

It is said that when you are older you can remember events that occurred years before more vividly than you could even a day or two after you experienced them. It seems true. I can no longer remember the exact moment I started writing this. But I can remember, in precise detail, the expression on Tal's face the moment he lost the mowing bag. It was partially a look of frustration, but mostly fear. Perhaps he was worried that his father would find out and take it out on him or Kyle as he'd done before, or maybe he was scared because Kyle had told him not to screw up and he'd let him down, proven he could not be trusted.

In the newspaper article, the hole is only twelve feet deep; they'd had it measured afterward. But in my memory it is deeper. The bag is at the very bottom, we know that, but even on our bellies Tal and I cannot make out its shape in the darkness. Warm fumes leak from the hole, making us a little dizzy and our eyes water, a dank odor, the scent of black syrupy grass that has been decomposing for more than a decade. Tal has a flashlight and I am holding the ladder we've carried from his garage. If Tal is nervous or even hesitant as we slide the ladder into the hole, he does not show it—he is not thinking about the lizard creatures from the swamp or anything else that might be down there. Perhaps he imagines there is nothing below but ten summers' worth of grass, waiting like a soft bed of hay.

We both stare into the hole for a moment, then Tal mounts the ladder carefully, the flashlight clamped between his teeth, and just before his mop of blond hair disappears, he glances at me and smiles—almost like he knows what is going to happen next.

A few seconds later I hear him say, "It smells like shit down here!" He says something else and laughs, but I can't hear what it is.

The flashlight never goes on. Not after I yell to him. Not after I throw sticks and tiny stones into the hole and tell him to stop fooling around. Not even after I stand in the light of the opening and threaten to take a whiz on him—even pull down my bathing suit to show him I am serious—not even then does it go on.

Later, in the tenth grade, a few years after my family had moved to Pennsylvania, I received a letter from Kyle Walker. He was living and working in Raleigh since high school. In the letter, he said he wanted to know what had happened that day. He'd always meant to ask me, but could never bring himself to do it. There was no one else who had actually been there, and it would help him out if he knew the details.

A few days later I wrote him a long letter in which I described everything in detail. I even included my own thoughts and a little bit about the dreams I had. At the end I said I would like to see him sometime if he ever made it to Pennsylvania. The letter sat on my bureau for a few weeks, but I never mailed it. I just looked at it as I went in and out of my room. After a month I put it back in my desk drawer.

Two firemen die in the attempt to rescue Tal. Two others end up with severe brain damage before the fire chief decides that they are looking at some *seriously* toxic fumes and are going to have to use oxygen masks and dig their way in from the sides. Later the local newspaper will say that Tal and the two firemen had probably lived about half an hour down there, that the carbon dioxide had only knocked them out at first, but that the suffocation had probably been gradual.

There is a crowd of people watching by the time the young firemen carry out Tal's body and strap it onto the stretcher. He no longer seems like someone I know. The skin on his face is a grayish blue color, and his eyes are closed like he's taking a nap. Seeing Tal this way sends Kyle into the small patch of woods on the other side of the house. Later that night Kyle will have to tell his parents, just back from their fishing trip at Eagle Lake, what has happened. There will be some screaming on the back porch and then Kyle will go into his room and not come out. For years everyone will talk about how hard it must have been on him, having to carry that type of weight so early in life.

When the last of the ambulances leave, my mother takes me home and I don't cry until late that night after everyone has gone to sleep, and then it doesn't stop. Tal's parents never speak to me again. Not even at the funeral. If they had, I might have told them what I sometimes know to be the truth in my dream: that it was me, and not Tal, who let the mowing bag slip into the hole. Or other times, that I pushed him in. Or once: that I forced him down on a dare.

That is the real story, I might say to them. But I will not tell them about the other part of my dream. The part where I go into the hole, and Tal lives.

coyotes

MY FATHER IS A FAILED documentary filmmaker. I say failed because he made only one film in his life. But for a short time in the late seventies, when I was growing up, he achieved what he would later refer to as moderate fame. The source of his moderate fame was a short documentary film about a group of Shoshone Indians living in southern Nevada. I doubt that anybody remembers the film now, but in the weeks and months that followed its release, my father received critical acclaim at several small film festivals, earned some grant money, and garnered enough hope and courage to continue making films for another ten years. To my knowledge, he never completed another film after that, but instead spent the next ten years of his life jumping around from one project to the next, shooting for several weeks or months, then eventually abandoning the current film for another that he believed had more potential.

My mother and I were living in southern California, where she worked as a lawyer, and every few months my father would call from a different part of the country with news of his latest concept—it was always his best yet—and ask my mother to sell something of his, or cash a bond, or take out another mortgage on the house. And finally, when there was nothing left to sell, he began to simply ask her for loans. Technically my parents were separated by then, but my mother was still very much in love with him, never stopped loving him, and worse, she believed with an almost stubborn myopia in his talent. She wanted my father to succeed, perhaps even more than he did, and to this day I still think this was her greatest flaw.

I can say now, twenty years later, that my father was never destined for the type of fame he once hoped to achieve. He was never meant to be a great filmmaker (few documentarians are), and he was never meant to receive even the lesser distinctions that so many of his contemporaries enjoyed. The small amount of talent he did possess only seemed to serve as a source of frustration for him, a constant reminder of some vague, unrealized potential. But at the time— this was in my early childhood—I believed fully in his potential, and though I missed him dearly, I never once faulted him for being away so often. By the time I was twelve, my mother and I had become more or less accustomed to his absence in our lives. We were used to the way he showed up every few months to edit film stock, the way he promised each time that he would come home more often, and the way he would then leave, a week or so later, just as suddenly as he'd arrived. The few months each year that my father was home, he would spend down in our basement, buried in film stock, researching his next project or sometimes editing footage from past projects he planned to resume. The basement became his refuge. His designated workspace and also his bedroom since my parents had separated. When he was not down there, he kept the door locked at all times, and though it seems strange to admit now, in all the years we lived in that house, I can still remember only one occasion when my father actually allowed me down there. It was the winter I was ten. My father had needed some help carrying some boxes up the stairs, and after several loads, he simply thanked me, patted me on the back, then turned around and locked the door behind him. That was it. I was only down there a matter of minutes, but from what I remember it was nothing special, just a small dark space filled with dusty film equipment. There was a narrow cot in one corner, a few bookcases against the wall. But the rest of the room was just a cluttered pile of old cameras and microphones, editing machines and cardboard boxes, all marked and containing what I assumed to be reels and reels of undeveloped film stock.

In the evenings—that is, the evenings my father was home—I would spend long hours at the kitchen table, paging through my assigned reading, listening to the click of the editing machine below me. At the time, I was still too young to resent him or hold him accountable for being away so much. Instead, I filled the space he had left in our lives with an idealized image of him: a man on the verge of great fame, a man I would one day be able to brag about. I imagined myself walking into school with a picture of him on the cover of a national magazine. I imagined the large house we would one day own—a large split-level structure up in the Hollywood Hills, a mansion with palm trees and a lit swimming pool in the backyard. And when I found myself bored with my schoolwork, I would walk over to the other side of the kitchen and study the small article my mother kept framed on the wall. The article was about my father's first film, and though most of the review was favorable, there was one short sentence that always got me—a sentence near the end of the article in which the critic described my father's film as "the unmistakable work of young genius." In the years since, I have come to realize that it was probably those words and the weight they carried that allowed me to forgive him for so long. Perched at the kitchen table, I would repeat them in my head like a mantra. I must have believed that if I said them enough times, if I copied their cadence, they would come true.

The summer I want to talk about—the summer I turned thirteen— my father returned one evening after a six-month shoot in the flat and barren deserts of west Texas. He had been away almost all of the previous year, filming and interviewing migrant workers who lived a few miles north of the Mexican border. He was working on a film about illegal immigration at the time, approaching it from the perspective of the immigrants. But he ran into some legal complications, I think, and also became frustrated by the workers' unwillingness to be filmed. It had been years since my father had been able to afford a crew. He worked now almost entirely out of the back of his van, storing his cameras and equipment in the cargo space and sleeping in a small tent next to the back door. Earlier in the summer he had come home for a long weekend to edit the small amount of footage he had collected, and then several weeks later, depressed and discouraged, he had come back again. I don't know what it was that compelled my father to come back from Texas that second time. Maybe he saw something down there that frightened him. Or maybe he just came to a point where he'd been away from us too long. All I know is that he ended up driving for three days nonstop, pulling over only to sleep, and when he finally arrived at my mother's house he was so tired he could barely stand. To make matters worse, the night he showed up unannounced, my mother was entertaining a man—a colleague of hers from the firm, a lean older gentleman named David Stone.

The three of us were sitting around the kitchen table when my father showed up looking strung out and disheveled from three days on the road. His face was still unshaven, and there was a large army surplus bag slung over his right shoulder. By then I had become accustomed to these sudden, unexpected arrivals. No phone call or letter. No prior notice of his plans. Just my father—bleary eyed and sleep deprived—appearing with a duffel bag at our door. I could see the genuine alarm in David's face, but before he could stand up, my mother touched his hand gently and smiled. Then she stood up and hugged my father.

"You're back," she said, trying not to seem surprised.

"I'm back." He smiled.

Over her shoulder, my father winked at me, then regarded David. The two men's eyes met briefly, then my father slowly released my mother.

"This is David Stone," my mother said, motioning toward the far end of the table where David was sitting, blank faced.

"Nice to meet you." My father smiled.

"Likewise," David nodded. My father said a few more things about his trip—how his van had broken down twice in Albuquerque, how he'd spent the better part of a day in El Paso—and then, claiming to be exhausted, he headed straight downstairs to the basement.

After he left, my mother looked at David and shrugged. David nodded, as if to say he understood, and then a moment later she walked him to the door.

At the time, none of this seemed unusual to me. My mother had always dated other men while my father was away, and my father had always seemed to understand this. I don't think he ever really worried about it. Like me, he seemed to understand that my mother never took any of these men that seriously. They were always the same type: soft spoken and bookish. Men who made few demands of her time and accepted whatever terms she presented. Men who she would later describe as "perfectly fine" or "innocuous, but a little dull." None of these guys would ever last longer than a few dates before my mother would get bored and cut them loose. But David Stone was different somehow. He was tall and handsome, an ex–air force pilot who was now one of the senior partners at my mother's firm. He had gone to Stanford Law School and traveled around Europe as a young man, and though I don't think my mother was in love with him, she didn't break things off with him either. It's possible that she just wanted to make my father jealous, or perhaps she wanted to let him know that she was moving on with her life and would not be waiting around for him anymore. Whatever the reason, she continued to go out with David in the evenings after work and my father continued to stay in the house, quietly editing film stock in our basement.

I have few memories of my father during that time. He stayed down in the basement even more than usual, working ten hours a day, emerging only for the occasional meal. The few evenings that we ate together as a family, he seemed distracted, on edge, talking at length about his project and what he believed to be the "real problem" with illegal immigration. He talked nonstop, and when my mother would break in to say that she was running late, my father would pretend to ignore her. "This problem isn't going away," he would say to no one in particular. "It's not going anywhere."

"Well, I have to go somewhere," she'd smile. "And I'm late."

My father never inquired about where my mother went in the evenings, or what she did. I think he was just trying his best to be supportive and understanding. But I also think that he was having trouble with the fact that my mother now had a serious boyfriend, and that this boyfriend drove an Aston Martin and had offered to take my mother and me to a small island off the coast of Mexico. He didn't talk about these things, though. He kept whatever he was feeling inside to himself. And when my mother mentioned David in conversation, he would simply nod and wait for her to change the subject. There was only one evening that I can remember my father even acknowledging David's existence. It was the night after my first swim meet of the summer. We were sitting around the table, my father smoking cigarettes, my mother reading over her cases for the next day, and somehow the subject got around to a case David was working on. My father seemed to think that David was misrepresenting his client. He seemed to think that there was something reprehensible about the way David was approaching the case, and before long, he was launching into a series of vague assertions about David's character.

My mother listened patiently, neither defending David nor acknowledging the deficiencies that my father seemed to think he possessed. I could see that she wasn't going to let my father coerce her into bad-mouthing him. But at the same time, I don't think she wanted a fight. So she just sat there with a bemused smile on her face, and when my father finally asked her what she really knew about this character anyway, she shrugged and said "There's not much to know. David's a pretty simple fellow. Never strayed far from the path, if you know what I mean."

My father nodded. Then he looked out the window and lit a cigarette. "He's got money," he said after a moment. "That must be nice."

My mother laughed. "Must be," she said. "I wouldn't know."

"No," he said. "I guess you wouldn't."

My mother looked at her watch then. "Yikes, I'm late," she said. "Will you boys take care of the dishes?"

I told her we would.

My father shrugged.

My mother stood up then, and as she crossed the kitchen, my father looked at her with the gravity of a troubled father addressing his only daughter. "Just remember," he said. "It's the ones who appear simple that turn out to not be so simple in the long run."

"I'll keep that in mind." My mother smiled and then she walked out of the room.

As soon as my mother went into her room to get ready for her date, my father went down to the basement, cranked up one of his rare recordings of Bartók, and proceeded to get stoned by himself. Left to clean the dinner dishes, I stood dutifully at the sink, scrubbing the plates in their porcelain bed, listening to the pulse of the music below me, the frantic whir of the editing machine. On nights like this, my father would stay down there for hours, pretending to work, but really just waiting for the sound of my mother's car in the driveway. Hours later, when the front door opened, he would emerge from his subterranean bedroom and follow her upstairs. From my own room across the hall, I would hear him talking to her and sometimes even crying. And though I know that she loved him deeply and that some nights she even let him stay with her in her room, my mother also knew better than to get back together with him. I don't even know if that was what my father had wanted, only that after two weeks of watching her disappear in the evenings, after two weeks of listening to David's car pull into our driveway, he announced that despite his earlier plans, he would be returning to Texas to finish his project. We were sitting around the dinner table when he brought it up.

I expected my mother to say something then, to protest as she usually did, but instead she just stood up and began to do the dishes.

"When are you coming back?" I asked.

"I can't really say for sure," he said, staring at my mother's back. "It might be a while this time."

"Six months?" I said.

"Six months," he said. "Possibly a year. It's hard to say."

"A year?" I said.

He shrugged. "Could be."

"Well just let us know," my mother said from the sink, without turning around.

"I'll do that," my father said.

He rose from the table then and remained standing in the middle of the kitchen for some time. It seemed like he was waiting for my mother to turn around. But she never did, and after a few minutes he headed down to the basement. The next morning, as the fog was burning off the ocean, I watched his van pull out of the driveway.

In the evenings that summer, you could sometimes hear coyotes in the hills above our neighborhood. When my mother was out with David, I would often sit on the roof outside my bedroom window and listen for the ones that lived on the steep slope behind our house. You never saw these creatures during the day, but at night, after the sun had descended at the far end of our street, you could sometimes hear them howling, like dogs, in the distance. Across our back lawn, you could see the dark ocean, silvered in moonlight, and beyond that the lights from the tiny houses in the marina. It seemed that I had spent my entire childhood on that roof, staring out at the water, believing that if I stared long enough I might be able to discover something meaningful about the way the world worked.

At the time, I only had one friend—a very thin Vietnamese boy named Chau Nguyen—and in the evenings after dinner, Chau would sometimes join me on the roof outside my window. Chau and I swam together on the swim team, and sat next to each other in school, but despite our closeness in age—he was only a year older—he claimed to have a lot more of what he called "vast worldly experience." He had grown up in Vietnam and he liked to tell long and elaborate tales about all the things he had done over there. How he had once been allowed to carry a machete in school and how he had cut people with that machete when they'd mouthed off to him. I knew that most of his stories were flat-out lies, but he had told them so many times and in such vivid detail that half the time I found myself believing them. Chau's favorite stories, of course, were those that involved women. He once told me that he had six girlfriends back in Vietnam, and that it had taken great skill to manage so many at once. Other times he would talk about the teenage prostitutes—the *thanh ngoài*—who he claimed to visit regularly. And yet, for all of his vast worldly experience, for all of his macho bravado and sexual expertise, Chau was still a bed wetter, and for this reason my mother was always reluctant to let him spend the night. I would plead with her—promising that it would never happen again—but she would always come up with some excuse for why it just wasn't a good night for Chau to stay over. This went on for most of the summer, but then one evening toward the middle of July, as a compromise, she brought home a special protective sheet, a plastic drape, which she made me attach under the regular sheet on Chau's bed. Chau never said anything to me about this sheet, but I imagine he must have felt it. This was midsummer, a week or so after my father had left town. It was the same evening that David showed up at our front door in a tux, wanting to take my mother to a formal party up in Newport Beach. David had rented a limo that night and bought an expensive bottle of wine, and for a few hours before the party, he and my mother drank and laughed out on the back patio, while Chau and I ate frozen pizzas in front of the TV.

Later, after my mother and David had left for the party, Chau and I took what was left of their wine out onto the roof and listened for coyotes. It was warm out that night, the sun descending at the far end of the street, and we talked for a long time about what we'd do if we ever saw one. How we believed we could tame them like regular dogs, and let them sleep in our rooms. We stayed up late. Chau had brought a pack of Malaysian cigarettes that he'd stolen from his grandfather's bedroom, and we smoked each and every one. Later, after he had fallen asleep, I got out of my bed and crawled back onto the roof. Out of habit I never went to bed before my mother got home from her dates. I had convinced myself that it was my duty to wait up for her—to watch over and protect the house—but in reality, it was just hard for me to fall asleep before I heard the sound of her car in the driveway. That night I remained on the roof for several hours, watching patiently for the headlights of the limousine, staring out at the ocean, silvered in moonlight. I wanted to be there when she returned, I wanted to see her expression when she walked to the door. But eventually boredom got the better of me and I went back inside and walked downstairs to get some water. The house was chilly that evening. There was a breeze moving through the air, and as I crossed through the living room into the kitchen I saw what I believed to be the shadowy shape of my father, hunched over the kitchen table, writing in a spiral notebook. As near as I could tell he had wandered into a dream I was having. Or I had wandered into a dream he was having. The patio door was open behind him, and the wind was blowing into the house. He looked up when he saw me, smiled, then went back to writing. I didn't say anything at first. I just stood there, my mind not quite processing how he could be in our kitchen. After a moment, he tore the paper out of the notebook, put it in an envelope, and handed it to me.

"I want you to give this to your mother," he said.

I stared at him. "I thought you were in Texas," I said.

"Not yet," he said. "I've been staying in town. I couldn't leave at first, but now I can." He put his hand on my shoulder. "I'm making a clean break this time."

"A clean break?"

He nodded.

I didn't understand what he meant by a clean break, but I sensed intuitively that he would not be returning for a while.

"Do you want to come with me?" he said after a moment. It was the first time my father had ever opened such an invitation to me, and though a part of me wanted to say yes, I knew that my mother would never forgive me if I did.

"I have swim team," I said.

My father nodded. "Swim team," he smiled. "Oh yes. Right. Of course." Then, as if that would forever explain the difference between us, he patted my shoulder and disappeared through the sliding glass doors.

Even now, fifteen years later, my mother and I have never spoken about that letter. After my father left, I just placed it on the counter, and the next morning when Chau and I came downstairs for breakfast, it was gone.

In the days that followed, I tried to look for signs in my mother's face that would reveal what my father had written. But she seemed the same—neither excited nor despondent—simply content with whatever terms he had left on. She continued to go out with David in the evenings, and on the weekends she went with him to parties in various beach towns up and down the coast. These parties often ran late. Some nights she wouldn't return until the early hours of the morning. And yet I continued to wait up for her as I always had, stubbornly hopeful that one night she might return distressed and teary eyed, resigned to the fact that things with David were never going to work.

Maybe if I had known what my mother was going through that summer, I would have been more sympathetic. Maybe I would have forgiven her for staying out all night with David or for not calling my father on the weekends as she used to. But I didn't, so I began to purposely put a distance between us. I began staying late at swim practice, eating dinner with Chau's family, taking late night walks along the beach by myself. I had convinced myself that my mother was somehow trying to hurt my father by dating David. I held her responsible for driving him away, for all the days that had passed with no word from him. It seemed to me that she was somehow trying to replace my father, and I worried that the rest of my life would be spent on the outside: watching my mother and David leave in the evenings, waiting for hours until they returned. The truth was, I didn't like David. To me, he was just like all the other men my mother dated, full of false flattery and phony affection. The only difference was that he was slightly better looking, and perhaps a little better off financially, and maybe a little more polite, but otherwise he was unexceptional, and I believed that my mother must have known this too.

Some evenings, while she was changing in her room, David would sit with me out on the patio and ask me questions. He would inquire about my performance on the swim team or my friends at school, and sometimes, when he was tired of my one-word answers, he would simply talk about himself. Before becoming a prosecuting attorney, David had been in the air force and he liked to talk about all the places he had flown over. How he'd been stationed in Southeast Asia during the tail end of the Vietnam War, and how he still thought about that time in his life without regret. He spoke about the war almost romantically, as if it had happened just the other day, and I would think then about Chau's family—his uncle who had been killed on a jungle road late one night, returning from his girlfriend's house in a neighboring town.

"Did you ever kill anyone?" I asked David one night when he was over for dinner.

My mother gave me a look.

"No," he said. "We were pulling out by the time I got over there. It was all over by then, chief."

"But you would have," I said. "If they had asked you to?"

"Alex," my mother said.

"I want to know," I said.

My mother stood up then and walked over to the sink. "I want you to go to bed," she said to me.

"I want him to answer."

She turned then and stared at me, but I didn't move. I kept looking at David. He sipped his coffee slowly, then looked at me in a way that told me we were never going to be friends.

"Yes," he said. "I would have."

It would be years before I learned everything that went on between my mother and father that summer. I didn't know then that my father's mind was slowly unraveling. I didn't know that all this time he had been "away," he'd really been staying at a motel in town. I didn't know that my mother still spoke to him on the phone or that she went to see him in the evenings after work. What I did know was that things were changing irreversibly in our lives. And what I remember is that one evening after one of my swim meets, as Chau and I were pedaling home on our bikes, I spotted my father's blue van on the street outside our house. The motor was running, and as I coasted up next to the passenger-side door, my father winked at me and smiled. I could see that he'd broken the edge of his front tooth.

"Hop in," he said.

I stared at him.

"Take a load off, compadre."

"Where are we going?" I asked.

"Well, that's where I'm going to be needing your help."

I coasted my bike over to the driveway and dropped it on the front lawn, then raced back to the van. I turned to wave to Chau, who was sitting on his bike, confused.

My father leaned over and unlatched the passenger door.

"What happened to Texas?" I said, climbing into the front seat.

"Still there as far as I know," he smiled.

"I mean, why aren't you there?"

"Long story," he said.

"Have you been here the whole time?"

"What do you mean?"

"Have you been here in town?"

My father shook his head. "I went back," he said. "I was in Texas for a while, but then I ran out of money. That's what I need to talk to your mother about."

As we drove, my father explained that he needed directions to the new firm where my mother was working. He said that he needed to discuss some "issues of finance" with her. He stared at the road the whole time, expressionless, and I could tell by the way he wouldn't look at me, the way he wouldn't turn his head, that he was lying. I had a sense that he hadn't gone anywhere. But I nodded anyway, and then told him the quickest way to get to my mother's new firm. He smoked as he drove, and from time to time, he'd look at me and wink. At a stoplight, he put his hand on my shoulder.

"I'm curious," he said. "You think you'd ever like to do something like this for a living?"

"Like what?" I said.

"Like what I do."

"You mean, make movies?"

"Films," he said.

"Films."

"Right."

"I don't know," I said.

He laughed. "Well, I wouldn't," he said. "Not if you can help it."

"What do you mean?" I said.

But he didn't answer me. He just smiled. When the light changed, he dropped his cigarette out the window and touched my arm. "Are you okay?" he asked.

"Yes," I said. "I'm fine."

It was dark by the time we finally pulled into the empty parking lot of the firm. My father parked next to the building, beneath a banyan tree, and turned off the engine. I could see that the light in my mother's second-floor office was still on, and when she came to the window and stood there, I realized that my father had not come to see her about money at all. He didn't even seem to want her to know we were down there. He leaned back in his seat, his face hidden in shadow, and as she stood in front of the window in her navy skirt, talking on the phone, I sensed that my father was not seeing the successful attorney my mother had become. I sensed that he was seeing the nineteen-year-old girl he had married, the art student at Berkeley, the star of all his student films, his sole crew member for several years—because he turned to me then and smiled. He said, "There will never be anyone in your life as beautiful as your mother."

I nodded.

"Remember that," he said, putting his hand on my shoulder. "If you don't remember anything else, remember that."

A moment later, my mother hung up the phone, and as she was packing up her briefcase, I saw David walk into her office. David was holding a stack of papers, legal documents I guess, and as he stood in front of her, talking, my mother sat up on her desk. She said something to him, then he walked over and hugged her. I saw him place his hand on her hip. I saw my mother smile. Then she leaned into him and kissed his neck. They remained like that, embracing, for what seemed like a long time. I had stopped watching by then. I was looking instead at my father, whose face seemed to have lost all its color. He was biting down on the side of his lower lip, and I worried that he might start to cry. But instead he just said, "Explain this to me, son."

I shrugged.

"Can you explain this to me?"

I shook my head. "No," I said. "I can't."

He rubbed his face, then rolled down his window and started up the van. I saw him glance up at the window one more time, then shift into gear.

"Have you seen enough?" he asked, without looking at me.

I told him I had.

That night, driving along the ocean road, my father talked to me as if I were a grown man, as if I were his father. He spoke to me as if he expected me to provide an answer to something he was trying to figure out. But I was too angry to listen to him. I was not angry for what he'd made me see, but for implicating me in his plan. I worried that my mother would find out, and see my assistance as a betrayal. For the first time in my life, I didn't want to be aligned with him. For the first time I found myself wishing that he had been a different man. Maybe if I had known that it would be years before I saw him again, I might have treated him differently. But I didn't, so I stared out the window at the ocean, ignoring his questions until he finally stopped asking them.

When he dropped me off at home that night I imagined that he went back to his motel room by the ocean. I imagined that he maybe had a beer and then went to sleep. I went up to my own room and then out to the roof where I sat, listening for coyotes. I sat out there for a long time, and it wasn't until later that night, when my mother came bursting through the front door in hysterics, that I realized my father had gone back to the firm. From where I was perched on the roof, I could hear her crying as she stumbled into the house. I ran downstairs to the kitchen and found her sitting at the table, her face cupped in her hands.

"Mom," I said.

But she wouldn't look at me. Her left hand was bleeding through a paper towel.

"Are you cut?"

She shook her head, still looking down.

"Mom," I said. "What the fuck happened?"

Over the years my mother has told me different versions of the story. In one version my father simply pushed David around and threatened him. But in other versions my mother would imply that it had become more violent than that. Years later she would explain that the police had had to come to break things up, that they'd taken my father away and called an ambulance for David. She would shake her head. She would stop for a moment and look at me. "It's the worst thing in life," she would say. "It's the worst thing in life to see someone you love reduced to that."

After that night it was several years before I saw my father again. My mother kept his whereabouts hidden from me until I was in high school, explaining only that he was going through a difficult period and that it would be best for everyone if I didn't see him. I know now that my father spent some of that time in a Los Angeles hospital, where he was treated for severe depression, and then, after that, in a halfway house in Pasadena. In the years since, I have heard from him only occasionally—phone calls on my birthday or Christmas—but even these brief conversations have become less and less frequent as time has passed. I don't resent him now in the same way I did as a teenager. I know that what happened to him was not in his control, and though I know she still holds herself accountable, I don't blame my mother either. Still, it bothers me that I have never seen the one film my father finished. He keeps the original print in a safety deposit box somewhere in Los Angeles, and though I have asked him about it on more than one occasion, he will not show it to me. From what my mother has told me, the film is about the spiritual beliefs of the Shoshone Indians, the way they believe that the physical world and the spiritual world are closely connected, almost coexisting, and it is, according to her, the most visually stunning film she has ever seen. There is a picture I have in my living room of my father and her on the night of the premiere. They are standing outside a small theater in New York City, and my father is pointing above him at the lights of the marquee. It is the only time in my life that I can remember seeing my father in a suit, and my mother, next to him, in a long evening gown. They are holding each other and smiling, the two of them, leaning slightly into the wind, bracing themselves against something they cannot yet see.

azul

TONIGHT I'M DRIVING our exchange student, Azul, to his lover's house on the other side of town. Azul has been seeing this boy Ramón for the past three months, and though I am not entirely thrilled about the idea, each Friday night I drive him across town to see him. Azul never talks to me during these trips, never even acknowledges my presence, but when we pull up close to Ramón's apartment he begins to check his face in the mirror, begins to comb his hair and straighten his shirt. He smiles at me briefly before turning his head toward the window and looking out at the long row of palm trees that line the street. He has told me on more than one occasion that he and Ramón are just friends, but I know from my wife, Karen, that this is just a front, that he and Ramón have been seeing each other romantically for almost a month.

I don't press the issue with Azul. I know that technically he has not come out to the other kids at his high school, and I know that even if he did want to tell me, he wouldn't feel comfortable bringing it up. He is much closer with Karen, who he has begun to call Mamá and who he now takes a photography course with once a week in the evenings. They stay up late at night, talking in the kitchen, sharing jokes and laughing. Sometimes I get the sense that Karen has become closer with Azul than she is with me. And yet, when it comes down to driving him across town to see Ramón it is always me who Azul asks. It is our only time alone together, though most nights, like tonight, he is too distracted to even look at me.

Tonight he stares absently out the window as I turn the radio dial, searching for a station that meets his approval.

"Stop," he says, when I hit a Latin techno station. Then he smiles and nods his head. "Listen," he says. "Listen, Paul."

I wonder sometimes what his parents would think of me driving their son across town to spend the weekend with a boy I've never met. Karen and I have had countless fights on this subject, and though I usually end up losing these fights, surrendering to her notion that Azul is a grown man and that if it were a girl, not a boy, I was taking him to see, I wouldn't have a problem with it, I still wonder.

"They're safe," Karen assured me the other night, as we lay in bed. Then she reminded me that I was doing the exact same thing at his age. "He's eighteen years old," she said. "He's in love." She took my hand and held it. "He's not an idiot, Paul."

Ramón Cruz is waiting in his doorway when we pull up to the small lawn outside his house. Six feet tall and lanky, Ramón Cruz dwarfs Azul by almost a foot. Azul climbs out of the car and walks over to greet him. They stand for a moment and hug, then Azul turns to me and waves.

"Thanks, Paul," he yells. "I'll be in touch."

"Okay." I yell back, then I smile at Ramón Cruz, who is standing at the door. He looks at me and nods. Then he puts his arm around Azul and leads him back inside.

Originally it was Karen's idea to host an exchange student. She said that she thought it would be good for us, that being childless for almost a decade had made us distant, though she was careful not to blame me when she said this. I know that she does blame me, partly, for the fact we have never had kids. But I also know that she has always been mindful not to let me know that she feels this way. It doesn't really bother me anymore. When the doctor first told me that I would never be able to impregnate my wife, I got drunk for a week straight, we both did, then I said to Karen, "You can leave me right now, and I'll never blame you. You can leave me right now, and I'll never think a bad thing about you."

I meant every word of what I said.

But when we went to sleep that night Karen held onto me, held onto me like she had never held on before, and when we woke up the next morning, she was still holding on.

"I'm not leaving," she said, as we lay there in the still darkness of our room. And she never did.

I admire her for staying when so many other women might not have. I will always love her for that. But I also know that she has never fully given up on the idea of having kids. We considered adoption at one point, but somehow the idea of it never settled with us. We could never really imagine bringing up a child that was not our own. And so it was surprising to me last spring when Karen came home from Rice, where she teaches part-time, with a handful of pamphlets and brochures. She laid them out in front of me on the counter and smiled.

"It's just for a year," she said. "We can think of it as an adventure."

"An adventure?"

"Or at least a distraction."

"A distraction from what?"

She looked at me and sighed. "Please, Paul," she said. "I want to do this."

Tonight Karen is out with some of her colleagues from the English Department at Rice, and when I get home I find the house dark and empty. I have begun to look forward to these long weekends alone, though I know that Karen misses Azul when he's not around. She has even suggested that Ramón stay with us a few times, a suggestion which Azul always meets with a groan. "Please, Mamá," he will say. "You *loca?*"

I fix myself a whiskey and Coke and walk out to the patio next to the pool. The air is warm, and I can smell the flowering scent of jacaranda trees in the neighboring yard.

Houston is not what it once was. I have lived here long enough to remember the oil boom, the way the town turned into a city overnight, and the way that just as easily it seemed to lose everything it had. I don't romanticize that time anymore, not in the way some people do, but I sometimes miss it, the energy in the air, the optimism and hope. It wasn't just the money that I liked. There was this sense that anything in the world was possible back then. You'd be sitting in a bar and some guy would walk up to you and hand you a hundred-dollar bill just because he liked the way you looked. And there would be this sense that it could be you, the next night, handing out hundred dollars bills to someone else.

I am turning this over in my head when the phone rings, and Karen is on the other end, telling me that her car has broken down.

"I'm in Montrose," she says. "Next to the museum."

"What happened?" I ask.

"I don't know," she says. "The engine just stalled, then all this smoke started coming out."

"Smoke?" I say. "What type of smoke?"

"I don't know," she says. "What do you want me to tell you? It was black smoke. *Smoke* smoke."

"Okay," I say. "Okay."

I pause for a moment and imagine her standing at a pay phone on the other side of the road. I imagine her crying.

"Paul?" she says.

"Yes."

"Can you come get me or what?"

When Karen and I first met she had just broken up with her first husband. He had been an academic, one of the many graduate professors she had dated at Yale, and during that whole first year in Houston she had told everyone she knew that she would never date another.

On our first date together, she told me that she loved the fact that I read mystery novels and Tolstoy with the same aplomb. She loved the fact that I went to Schwarzenegger films and watched football and didn't make a face when someone mispronounced the word *peripatetic*. "You're a natural," she said to me that night. "You're the real thing."

"As opposed to the 'unreal' thing?"

"Well, you're that too," she said. "But in a good way."

Her first marriage had seemed so fundamentally doomed to me that I had found it hard to listen to her when she talked about it. It had been a constant competition, she said. It had been fine up until she got her PhD. But then, as soon as she published her first article, as soon as she was offered the job at Rice, her husband all but stopped talking to her. It got ugly, she said. He would embarrass her publicly, at parties or lectures. He would correct her in front of his colleagues, or subtly hint at the gaps in her knowledge, as she tried to make a point. And so, when the job came through at Rice and he told her that she would have to stay, she left the East, left him, and moved to Houston.

She was still in her first semester when I met her through a mutual friend at a party. I can't remember too much about that party, but I do remember walking with her to her car, and then afterward, leaning with her against the side of a banyan tree as we kissed drunkenly beneath the stars.

A year later we were living together, and a year after that we were married. "I'm not getting married again," she told me on our wedding night. "So you better be sure. Because, like it or not, you're stuck with me."

"Is that a threat or a promise?" I asked.

"It's both," she said.

That night, when we get home from the garage, Karen tells me about Graydon Lear, the new Old English specialist in her department. She tells me that this Graydon Lear has a PhD from Harvard and that he has more publications than almost anyone in the department. She tells me that he is only twenty-eight years old and that he has been brought in, she believes, to replace her. I listen to her as she tells me about Graydon Lear's accomplishments, his promise, and the way that the other English professors hang on his every word. Then she tells me that next Wednesday night Graydon Lear will be giving a lecture on his latest book and that we *both* have to go. Generally, I try to beg off in these situations—I have been to one too many of these lectures in the past—but tonight I can see that she needs my support, so I take her hand and smile.

"Okay," I say. "Whatever you want."

Graydon Lear teaches his classes in a pair of old, ratty jeans and a T-shirt, she tells me after dinner. He goes to clubs with the graduate students and talks about the decline of punk rock during office hours. She has heard him playing his CDs at full blast, the heavy guitar licks echoing down the hall. And nobody, she says, nobody says a word.

"He sounds like a teenager," I say.

"He is," she says. "A very brilliant teenager."

On Sunday night Azul calls us from Ramón's house and Karen drives over to River Oaks to pick him up. They go out to the mall and afterward to a small restaurant in town. When they get home they are laughing, giggling about some shared joke, and Azul stands in the doorway and models his new shirt.

I am standing over by the stove, watching him, and as he turns to look at me, he begins to laugh. Then he stumbles backward and almost falls.

I look at Karen and she shrugs. I can tell that they've both been drinking. This has become a new development in their relationship. Whenever they go out, they drink. Azul has told Karen that at home his parents let him drink, and so Karen has decided that every once in a while it's okay if Azul has some wine with dinner, or a glass of beer after school. But I have never seen her let him get like this before.

"What is it, Paul?" Azul asks, though I can tell he is trying not to laugh.

I try to catch Karen's eye, but she is already going through the bags, pulling out pants and boxers, belts and shoes, asking Azul to try them on.

"All of it," she says. "I want to see *all* of it!"

Azul smiles coyly, pretends to be bashful, then takes the clothes and disappears down the hall.

For a second Karen and I are alone, and she smiles. It is a kind smile, a smile that says *relax*. But before she can say a word, I am heading down the hall and up the stairs.

Later, when Karen comes up to our room, she undresses in the dark, then slides up next to me under the sheets.

"He hates me," I say, as she rests her head on my chest. "I know he does."

"He doesn't hate you, hon. He's just a little scared of you."

"Well, isn't that the same thing?"

"No," she says. "It's not."

I look at her.

"You know, Paul," she says. "It's okay to relax once in a while. It's not a crime, you know."

"What's not a crime?" I say.

"Being happy," she says, taking my hand. "It's not a crime."

The next day, at Karen's suggestion, I take Azul to his photography class. She begs off, claiming that she has too much work to do, and though I can tell that Azul is not thrilled about the idea of going without her, he finally relents.

The photography class meets in a small classroom at HCC, the local community college, which is located just a few blocks from my old apartment and from the ad agency where I now work. There are about a half dozen people sitting around a small glass table when we arrive. The instructor, an older man, draws a diagram of a lens on the board and Azul takes notes. The man talks about apertures and light meters, and Azul nods earnestly. I sit there and stare at the new Pentax camera that Karen bought for him last month.

After class, I ask Azul if he feels like stopping for dinner on the way home. He shrugs and says, "Whatever you want, Paul."

He has not said a word to me the entire night, and I am beginning to realize that he is only going through the motions for Karen's sake.

"Do you like Vietnamese?" I ask, as we head up Alabama Avenue.

He shrugs. "I don't think so."

"Pizza?"

He shakes his head. "I guess I'm not so hungry."

"How about a drink?" I say. It is against my better judgment, but I begin to tell him about a bar that I know of, an old bar in the Heights that Karen and I used to go to when we were first married. "They have a pool table," I say.

Azul smiles, then shakes his head. "That's okay," he says. "I'm kind of tired."

I nod, and turn on the radio, and later, as we pull onto our street, Azul touches my shoulder and smiles.

He says, "You don't have to try so hard, Paul. I like you."

That night in bed Karen tells me that she has found a photograph of Ramón Cruz and a small bag of pot in Azul's desk drawer. She tells me that she hates herself for snooping, but she just couldn't help herself.

"What type of photograph?" I ask.

"It doesn't matter," she says, though I can tell that the content of this photograph has upset her.

"Maybe you should just forget about it," I say.

She nods, then rolls over on her back and sighs.

"Do you ever think about his parents?" she asks.

"His parents?" I say. "No. Not really."

"He never calls them," she says. "They always call here. Don't you think that's strange?"

"I don't know," I say. "I guess."

I remember then the photograph that Azul showed us on the night of his arrival, the photograph of his parents back in Belize. His father, a successful doctor, standing next to his mother, a grade school teacher, both of them lean and handsome, both of them devoted, you can tell, to their first and only son. I have spoken to his father only twice since then, and on both occasions it was awkward, the static on the line drowning out his voice. I look at Karen and I can tell that she is feeling some of that same guilt I sometimes feel on my long drives out to River Oaks.

"It's not so strange," I say, after a moment. "Think of yourself at eighteen."

"Oh God," she says. "Don't remind me."

"Well," I say. "That's my point."

She looks at me and shrugs. "I know," she says. "But still, I think it's strange."

Azul spends the next night at Ramón's house. We have never let him stay over on a weeknight before, but when he calls me from school, I find it hard to say no. It is strange, but it seems that I have never wanted to please anyone in my life as much as I want to please Azul at this moment. He says that Ramón will pick him up at school, and I say okay. Then he says, "Thanks, Paul," and hangs up.

When Karen comes home, I wait almost an hour before I bring it up.

"It's a school night," she says.

"I know."

I expect her to make more of a fuss, but she just opens up the fridge and takes out some wine. "He's mad at me," she says. "Did he say anything to you about it?"

"About what?"

"The pot."

"No," I say. "He didn't."

She looks at me. "I confronted him about it this morning."

"Oh yeah? And what did he say?"

"Well, nothing," she says. "Nothing at all. He just looked at me. He just looked at me and frowned. I think he hates me now."

"He loves you," I say, but she is already walking out the door and I don't think she hears.

Later on that night, as Karen works on her papers in the den, I stand at the kitchen counter and make us some dinner—a light dish of salmon and rice.

From the kitchen counter, I can see my wife huddled over the stack of student papers. She has been teaching at Rice for almost ten years, and yet has never been on track for tenure. They are still waiting for her to finish her book, a revised version of her graduate thesis, but Karen is no closer to finishing that book now than she was when I met her. She blames the heavy course load and the needy students, the excessive committee service they coax her into. But I haven't seen her sit down to write in almost a year. She is fearful, I think, fearful of what lies ahead. The department has already been making cutbacks and several of her colleagues—those who haven't published yet—are already being asked to leave.

"I'm next," she says to me. "I'm the last piece of dead weight."

"That's crazy," I tell her. "That's nuts." But I can see she's not assured.

After dinner, I do the dishes while Karen attends to her papers. When I finish, I bring her a cup of coffee on a tray.

"You're sweet," she says, as I place the coffee on her desk.

"I try," I say.

"I know you do," she says.

I sit down next to her on the couch.

"What do you think he's doing now?" she says after a moment.

"Who?"

"Azul. What do you think he's doing?"

"He's probably rolling up a fatty," I say.

"That's not funny."

"You're the one who got him drunk," I remind her.

"We had some wine with dinner," she says. "I did not get him *drunk*."

I lean my head on her shoulder, and ease my hand down her leg. We haven't made love in over a month, and I'm thinking: the wine, the music, *maybe*, but before I can make a move, she stands up and begins to clear her work.

"Maybe it was Ramón's pot," she says after a moment, staring out at the yard. "Maybe it was his, you know, and Azul was just holding it for him."

At school, Azul is popular. I know this because Karen tells me he is, and because boys like Azul are always popular. In all of his perfected straightness, he passes his classes with ease, flirts with the girls who are younger than him, and holds the second position on the boys' tennis team. Sometimes, when I pick him up at school, I see him standing in the middle of a group of girls, or off to the side of the tennis courts, making sly jokes with boys who are older than him, boys whose fathers run oil companies and banks, boys who I sometimes think would not say a word to him if they knew that he spent his weekends in a small stucco house with a boy named Ramón Cruz.

Azul is usually standing with these boys when I arrive, but today he is standing alone. He is upset, I can tell, and when he gets into the car, he simply turns on the radio and stares down at his hands. I want to say something to him, something to break the ice, but he doesn't seem to want to talk. When I bring up Ramón, he tells me that they are no longer talking to each other.

"And why is that?" I ask.

"Because he's a *maricón*," Azul says.

"A what?"

"A faggot," he says. Then he looks down before I can catch his eyes.

Later, Karen knocks on his door and I can hear them talking in soft whispers. First, I hear Azul crying, then I hear Karen soothing him. When she comes out, she takes my hand and leads me to our room. She closes the door behind us, sits down on the bed, and explains to me in a soft whisper that Azul and Ramón have broken up.

"Is he okay?" I ask.

"What do you think?"

I take her hand, and I think for a moment that we will kiss. But before I can say a word, she looks down.

"I thought we'd go to a movie tonight," she says.

"Okay," I say. "What do you want to see?"

"Not *us*," she says. "Me and Azul."

"Oh," I say. "Okay."

"I think he needs a distraction," she says, and then looks out the window.

"I thought he was the distraction," I say.

"Well, he is," she says. "Just not tonight."

Later that night, while Karen and Azul are at the movies, I go into Azul's room and look for his stash. After a little rummaging, I find a small bag hidden in the corner of his desk. I take it out and break off a small clump.

I haven't smoked pot since college, and it occurs to me as I roll the thin joint at the kitchen table that Karen has probably never smoked a joint in her life. I imagine her disapproval as I walk out to the pool and hit the lights. Then I ease down into the water and light the joint, and for a moment, supine in the pool, floating softly beneath the stars, I am weightless, mateless, lost.

It is Karen's idea to let Azul throw a party, and when she brings it up over breakfast, Azul jumps at the idea. Together they begin to form a list. It is amazing to me that Karen knows the names of the kids in Azul's class, that she knows who to invite and who not to. I can imagine my own mother in such a situation, being diplomatic and fair. Invite everyone, she would say. Why be mean? But Karen is not that type of mother. "Oh not her," she will say. Or, "Oh, I thought she wasn't so nice?" On the top of the "who not to invite" list, Azul has written Ramón's name in big bold letters. He has underlined it twice and put a special star in the margin. A star, Karen tells me later, means *absolutely not*.

That night in bed Karen lies awake, reading through her lecture notes for the following day. I have never seen her prepare so compulsively for a class before. Normally, she just goes in and wings it, talks off the cuff, as she says, but I can see that the fear of termination has made her nervous. She asks my opinion about the students, frets about what they might write in their final evaluations. Seeing her reduced to this state has begun to sadden me. I wonder if her early removal from this job might not be a good thing, a blessing in disguise. If the job makes her this unhappy, I think, why not drop it?

Later that night, as I stand outside of Azul's door, I can hear him talking to Ramón in a soft voice. I cannot make out a word that he's saying, but it is somehow comforting just to be there. From time to time I will hear him say something in Spanish or else simply sigh, and then I will move in slightly closer to the door. I imagine that all parents at some point in their lives go through something like this. I can imagine my own father standing outside of my door, listening to me talk to my friends about all the girls I'd never date. After a moment, I hear Karen's footsteps on the stairs and walk into the bathroom across the hall.

When I come out a minute later, she is standing outside of Azul's door, listening.

I take her hand. "Let's go to bed," I say.

At the lecture, Graydon Lear is dressed in khakis and a sports coat, his long hair pulled back in a neat, slick ponytail. Karen points him out to me as we sit down in the back row, then rolls her eyes, as if to say *just wait*. I am expecting him to seem young, to say something glib or irreverent, but as soon as he begins to speak, I am struck by the formality of his tone. He stands there at the podium and looks out at us, as if we are all just students in his class.

Like Karen, I was once an English major in college, and generally speaking I am able to follow about two-thirds of these lectures she takes me to, but tonight I am lost by the very first word. Graydon Lear is poised and charming. He makes clever puns and obscure jokes that gain chuckles from the crowd, but when he finishes, there is only awed silence, the communal acknowledgment that we are in the presence of greatness.

After the lecture, there is a small reception and Karen talks with some of her colleagues while I stand dutifully at her side, interjecting jokes at the appropriate moments and nodding, saying things like "very interesting" and "fascinating" a lot.

On the ride home, Karen is quiet and I know what she is thinking. I know that she is thinking about the chair, about the fact he didn't say a word to her the entire night. I know that she is thinking about her colleagues and the way they looked at her, the way they spoke to her in the commiserating tones of those who are in the know, those who in some short time will be the bearers of bad news. Even I noticed these things, and I think for a moment that this is why she brought me. To bear witness to her successor, her demise.

As we pull up on our street, Karen tells me that she expects to hear the bad news next week. That is when the contract renewals begin, she says. That is when the ax will fall. "I'm too old to be considered promising," she tells me. "Too old to be considered a wise and timely investment."

"They're assholes," I say to her. "Every one of them."

She looks at me and shakes her head. "I used to think I was smart," she says. "Not brilliant, but smart."

"How much wine have you had?"

She ignores me. "I mean, I know I'm not an idiot. But sometimes I feel like my mind is—I don't know. I feel like it's gone soft."

"Soft?"

"Like I've lost my edge." She looks at me. "I drift," she says. "Sometimes during class a student will be talking, and I'll be watching their lips move, but I won't be hearing them. I'm there, but I'm not there. Do you know what I mean?"

"You're the smartest person I know," I say. But I can tell she's not assured.

When we approach the house I can see that there is a long line of cars stretching down the street. These are nice cars, the types of cars my father would have called "foreign jobs." I count three or four SUVs before Karen turns to me and sighs.

"Can you imagine owning a Land Rover at seventeen?" she says.

"No," I say, taking her hand. "I can't imagine owning a Land Rover at forty-six."

Inside the house, we find a group of kids sitting in the hall, drinking beer. A few of them look up at us and smile, but the rest just turn away. Azul has told us that some of his classmates' parents allow the kids to drink in their homes. They all drop their car keys into a small, wooden bowl by the door, and as long as they don't try to leave, the parents let them drink as much as they want. Karen has never formally specified our policy on the whole drinking issue, but I can tell that she is not inclined to make a stand now. In general, neither of us likes to be the bad guy, especially where Azul is concerned, and so we just stand there and smile, and then we head outside to the yard, where we find Azul, slumped in one of the chaise lounge chairs by the pool.

"Hey, Mamá!" he shouts when he sees us, and then Karen walks over to greet him. I stand off in the shadows by myself and watch as Azul and Karen talk. I can tell by the expression on Karen's face that she is not giving him a lecture on underage drinking. Instead, my wife seems depressed and I can tell, as I watch her, that she is too discouraged, too disenchanted, too exhausted with her life, to tell anyone they can't do anything.

There are several ice-filled coolers by the pool, and after a minute, Azul walks over to one of them and hands Karen a beer. Karen twists the cap, holds the beer to her lips, then downs the whole thing like a champ.

Some of the kids beside the pool begin to laugh. "Shit," one of them yells. "Girl can drink!"

Azul puts his arm around Karen, and they stand there for a while, talking with the other kids. I wait for another minute or so. I am waiting for a sign from Karen—something in her eyes—but I never get one, so after a while I just turn around and head back in.

Inside the house, I find two young girls standing over a tray of shots in the kitchen. They are looking at each other and laughing. Then one of the girls—the shorter one—says, "Would you like one?"

"No thanks," I say.

"Are you sure?"

"Yes. I'm sure."

"Are you Azul's dad?" asks the other. "Not his dad, I mean—"

"Yes," I say. "Just for the year."

They smile.

"I'm on loan," I say, winking.

"Oh right," the taller girl says.

I want to say something else, something that will let them know that I am okay with the fact that they are drinking in my kitchen. But before I can say a word, they smile, shrug, and walk out of the room.

I stand in the kitchen and try not to feel old. I go to the fridge and discover that it has been taken over by bottles of Shiner Bock. I take one out, and then another, and then head upstairs to the bedroom.

I am almost shaking by the time I sit down on the edge of the bed. It seems amazing to me that I am allowing this to happen in my house—the house that I bought when I was twenty-eight—the house that Karen and I have poured half our paychecks into for the past ten years. I imagine drunken boys sprawled upon the new Persian carpet we bought last summer, dripping beer upon the tan leather couch we got last fall. I brace myself each time that there's a bang, certain it's one of our antique chairs splitting beneath the weight of a two-hundred-pound lacrosse player.

Around ten, the phone rings, and I hear Ramón's voice on the other end. It is rare that Ramón will call our house this late, and as I begin to explain to him that we are having a party, that *Azul* is having a party, I realize that I may in fact be drunk.

"Just tell him I called," Ramón says.

"Okay," I say. Then I pause. "You know, I can get him."

"No. That's okay."

"He wants to talk to you," I say, sounding suddenly more interested than I have a right to be.

"What?" Ramón says.

"Why don't you just come over," I say. "He'd like to see you."

There is a long silence. Then Ramón says, "I don't know." Then he says, "Did he say that?"

I realize then that I am getting ahead of myself here, that in truth I have no idea whether Azul wants to see him or not. I pause, and perhaps take too long to answer, because a moment later Ramón says, "Look, I'll just talk to him tomorrow, okay?" then hangs up.

I feel suddenly silly. I realize that there are close to fifty drunk teenagers in my house, and I am sitting here in the dark, half-drunk, trying to patch up the broken love life of my teenage exchange student. After a moment, I walk down the hall to Azul's room, hoping to find him there, but the room is empty. I go back to the drawer and find his stash—considerably smaller now—and break off another small clump. I take the rolling paper into the bathroom across the hall and roll myself a joint, pulling the smoke into my lungs as I run the shower at full blast. I consider the possibility that at the age of forty-six, I am beginning to develop a pot habit. This seems comical, then deeply, deeply sad.

I look at myself in the mirror. *Something ain't right here*, I say out loud.

Then there's a knock on the door. "Who's in there?" asks a girl.

"Just a second."

I take one last hit off the joint, flush the rest down the toilet, turn off the shower, then gargle with mouthwash before returning to the hall. I can tell that the girl can smell the cannabis on my breath because she just looks at me and smiles. "Hey," she says. "Got any more of that?"

"No," I say. "I don't."

Downstairs in the kitchen, I find Karen standing over a tray of shots, cutting limes. She holds the knife at me and says, "On guard!"

"You're drunk," I say.

"Ditto."

I want to tell her that she is wrong. That technically I am high, not drunk, but I can see that this is the type of information that might just in fact send her over the edge. So instead I just stand there and smile, assuming the stance of the pillar she wants me to be, and after a moment she takes my hand and smiles. "Hey," she says. "You know, some girl just got sick in our azalea bed."

"Oh yeah?" I say. "Well, two kids wanted to screw in our room."

"That right?"

"That's right."

"My goodness," she says. "This is all very wrong, isn't it?"

"It is," I say. "Reprehensible."

She laughs again. Then Azul comes into the kitchen from the living room, ready to collect the limes that she has sliced for his tequila shots.

"I don't want anyone driving home tonight," I say to Azul.

"No way, Paul," Azul smiles, pointing to a bowl on the other side of the kitchen, overflowing with keys.

"Good man," I say, trying to sound relaxed and jovial. But Azul is already out the door, and I am left there with Karen who simply smiles at me and says, "You are."

"What?" I say.

"A good man," she says. "You really are."

After that, I lose track of time. The party hits a crescendo around one or two, and then slowly, the kids—some of whom have brought sleeping bags, others just blankets—begin to pass out on the living room floor. It is dark in there, and I have no doubt that there is much groping, if not worse, so I stay clear of the room, remaining in the kitchen with a boy named Talbot, while Azul and Karen sit out by the pool with a small group of girls.

Talbot is telling me about his SAT scores. How he skipped one of the lines on the Scantron sheet, and how he was one off for every question after that. He got the lowest verbal score in the history of the school, he says, and though he has a 4.0 average and a 780 in math, Stanford has denied him early admission. He is nearly in tears by the time he finishes the story, and I have nothing much to say to him.

"My life is over," Talbot says. "I am eighteen years old, and my life is over."

"There are other schools besides Stanford," I say.

"Not for me," he says.

If I were not in an altered state at this moment, I might be able to say something comforting to him, something kind. But instead I just look at him and smile.

"Well," I say, "You can always transfer, you know. There's always that."

"Yeah," he says. "I guess."

It is some time later that night, as I am sitting in the kitchen with Talbot, listening to him talk about his ex-girlfriend in Dallas, that the doorbell rings, and a moment later Ramón Cruz appears.

I look at him and smile. "Glad you decided to come," I say.

He nods.

I point through the sliding glass doors to where Azul is sitting. "He's out there," I say.

Ramón nods again, then walks through the door.

"Who was that?" Talbot asks after Ramón has left.

"Oh, no one," I say. "Just a friend of Azul's."

"A friend?" he says. "Hmm." Then he smiles. "Hey, is there something going on between them?"

"Between who?"

"That dude and Azul."

"No, no," I say, sipping my beer. "No, I think they're just friends."

There was a short period of time just after we found out we could not have kids when I suspected Karen of cheating on me. This was in the winter of that year. Karen was busy at school, and things were slow for me at work. I was going home at lunch some days, just sitting around the house, watching TV, and Karen was coming home late. I knew that she had recently struck up a friendship with one of the new professors in her department, and I often suspected that she spent some of those evenings with him. She admitted once or twice to having coffee with him, and I began to imagine those coffees turning into dinners, and those dinners turning into something else. I had met this man once before, at a luncheon on campus, and he was not the type of guy you would normally feel threatened by. He was considerably older than Karen, nearing sixty, and he had just been divorced by his second wife. But still, his presence in Karen's life bothered me. He would call the house once or twice a week, and Karen would take the phone into her study and talk with him in a hushed whisper. Later, she would explain to me that he was very lonely, that he was having trouble accepting his recent divorce, and that she was the only friend he had. I never said anything at those moments. I was trying to be supportive. It was an especially vulnerable time in our marriage and I didn't want to bring my own fears and anxieties into the picture. But then one night, shortly after the spring break, Karen suggested bringing him with us on a trip down to Galveston, and I remember saying something insensitive then, something cold and dismissive, something about how maybe this guy needed to get some new friends. Karen looked at me then, and though I thought she was going to call me a cruel and heartless bastard, an insensitive jerk, she just nodded—maybe sensing my jealousy, maybe understanding my fear of loss—she just nodded, my beautiful wife, and said, "Well, yes, maybe you're right."

I don't know why it is that this memory returns to me at this exact moment, but for some reason I feel a sudden need to walk out to the yard and reclaim my wife. As I make my way out the door, however, what I see is not my wife, but a small group of girls huddled around Azul on the small concrete patio by the pool. They are holding him up and he is pretending to be unconscious, or dead, or so it seems, and for a moment I think that this is just a game, one of the many games that teenagers these days play. It is only when I get a little closer and see the blood that I realize it's not a game at all, and then all at once I feel it hit me. There is blood, unbelievable amounts of it, everywhere and as the girls slowly part I see my wife in the middle of the circle and she is holding Azul tightly and crying and then she begins to scream, scream like she is trying to get something out of her mouth but doesn't know how.

"What happened?" I say to one of the girls. "What the fuck happened?"

But they are just looking at Azul, slightly stunned, as if they are watching something in a movie and not something that is really happening and Azul is just lying there with his eyes closed, limp as a doll, and then this boy is on top of him and using his shirt to dab the blood, the unbelievable amount of blood that is coming, I can suddenly see, from his head.

"Somebody call a fucking ambulance!" says the boy, and then he looks at me as if this is suddenly my fault, and so I turn around and start back in, but by the time I reach the phone I can see that someone else has beat me to it. It is Talbot and he is talking in a frantic voice to the people on the other end. He looks at me with something like panic, maybe it is fear, but before he can say a word or even make a move, I am running over to the pantry and grabbing a wad of towels and then I'm running back out to the yard.

"Use these," I say, handing the boy the small bunch of towels and he immediately takes them and begins to apply pressure to Azul's head. By now most of the girls have scattered and the others are simply standing there, watching, and then I see my wife who is completely belly down on the lawn. I run over to her, but as I begin to pull her up she pushes me off and begins to cry. She seems almost like an animal at that moment, something inhuman and strange. The noises she is making are not noises I have ever heard another human being make.

"What happened?" I say when I get back to the boy, but the boy is too busy pushing the towels against Azul's head and it is not until some moments later that he finally looks up and says, "It was that fucking freak."

"Who?" I ask, and then suddenly I realize that Ramón is gone. I look around the yard, but he is nowhere in sight.

"Where did he go?" I ask.

But the boy doesn't answer. He just turns back to Azul.

Then he looks at me again and hands me a towel and I begin to help him. We work together, the two of us, and it is only after we have used up most of the towels and the blood has stopped, or at least slowed down, that I see the actual cut and realize it's not that big after all, not as bad as we thought.

"Hey, Paul," Azul says, when he finally opens his eyes. "What's happening?" He is trying to lift up his arm, but having trouble.

"How's it going, champ?"

"Not so good," he says. Then he says, "Where's Ramón?"

"I don't know," I say. "I think he left."

"Where did he go?" he asks, suddenly concerned. "How did he know—" But then he stops and doesn't finish.

"Should I call the cops?" asks the boy.

"I don't know," I say. "Did he hit you?" I ask Azul.

But Azul shakes his head. "I tripped," he says.

"That's bullshit," says the boy, "I saw that guy shove him."

"It was my fault," Azul says, adamantly, and then closes his eyes. I can feel his nails digging into my arm, and all at once I want to cry.

When the paramedics arrive a few minutes later, they walk over to Azul and hoist him up on a stretcher and then they talk to me and ask me what has happened, and I don't know what I tell them—I am talking so quickly and all the booze and the pot is mixing with my thoughts—but they seem to write it all down and then, when I finish, I ask them what will happen.

"What do you mean?" the taller one says.

"Is he going to be okay?" I ask.

"Well, it's hard to say," he says. "We'll need to run some tests, of course, but right now—it's just too early to tell."

"What about the blood?" I ask.

"What about it?" he says.

They ask me if I'm sober enough to drive and I tell them I'm not, and they just nod and say that they can take me in the ambulance with Azul, and I say that's fine, but first I need to get my wife, and it is then that I suddenly realize that in the midst of all this chaos I have somehow lost track of Karen, and it is only after I have run around the yard several times, calling out her name, pleading with her to join me, that I realize she is gone.

    I head over to the tool shed, then back around the side of the house, and then finally I see her out on the front lawn, standing on the curb, talking to the paramedics.

"How did this happen?" she says. "Who the hell invited Ramón to the party?"

"I don't know," I say, and all at once I want to tell her. I want to tell her the truth.

"I don't understand," she keeps saying. "I just don't understand." And then one of the paramedics comes over and tells us it's time to go.

"One of you is going to have to stay behind," he tells us. "We've only got room for one."

I look at Karen, and she nods.

"I will," she says, and turns away.

I walk over to her then and take her hand and pull her toward me and for a moment we just stand there, holding each other. It's going to be fine, I tell my wife, it's going to be fine. And she just nods and I can feel her body shaking in my arms, and I know that she is thinking about Azul and what will happen to him now, what we will tell his parents when they ask. I imagine his father, standing in his kitchen, the distant echo of his voice on the other end. It's going to be fine, I say again. It's just a cut. But I can feel the stiffness in her spine, the tension in her back. And it takes a while, almost several minutes, before we finally turn around and look at what we've done.

the theory
of light
and matter

IT WASN'T UNTIL THE LAST DAY of the fall semester that Robert finally spoke to me. I suppose, to be technical, he had spoken to me before then, since he was my teacher and he had called on me in class, but that was the first day that I can remember him looking up from his small wooden desk at the front of the room and saying my name. It was snowing that day and the quad outside the classroom was covered with a thin, white powder. The students who had arrived early were already sitting at their desks and when I walked into the room I remember Robert standing up by the front of the chalkboard, passing out our final exams. The exams he handed out that day contained a small equation typed neatly at the top of a blank piece of paper. There were no other markings, no directions, no words. Hours later, I would learn the origin of this equation, but at the time I simply understood that it involved a level of physics way beyond the comprehension of anyone in the room. Within an hour, I watched two of the brightest students in the class walk out the back door without handing in their work. Several others were simply looking up at Robert, as if they expected him to suddenly change his mind. But he made no movement, no gesture toward apology or remorse. He simply sat there, reading his book, and when the class period ended, when everyone except for me had departed in protest, Robert announced, in his soft, gentle voice, that my time was up.

"Heather," he said. "Please put down your pen."

Even now, ten years later, I find it hard to explain why I didn't leave then, why I instead walked straight up to the front of the room, handed Robert my exam, then stood there, stupidly, as he looked over my work. I suppose I had wanted him to say something encouraging to me, something kind, but after studying my work for what seemed like a long time, Robert simply stood, slid the small crumpled blue book into his satchel, and started for the door. And it was then, as he was putting on his coat and packing up his bag, that he turned to me, and in his soft, gentle voice asked me whether I would like to have some tea. It was the middle of winter, already a foot of snow on the ground, and though I easily could have, I did not imagine his invitation to be romantic. He was a frail man, thirty years my senior, and did not seem like the type who lured wide-eyed undergraduates back to his apartment.

"It's okay," he smiled. "I won't be hurt if you say no."

"No," I said, putting on my coat. "I'd like to have some tea."

As it turned out, we didn't have to walk far. It was only a short distance from the classroom to the small apartment Robert kept in town, and as we trudged awkwardly through the snow and ice, he asked me about my finals and what I planned to do over the Christmas break. The questions, I knew even then, were just a formality, but I appreciated the attention he gave to my answers, the cool and thoughtful way he responded each time that I spoke. He seemed to go out of his way to put me at ease, and the slightly nervous habit he had of glancing down whenever our eyes met made me feel strangely powerful. We had never really spoken before, not outside of class, and yet I already felt a calmness, a warmth in my blood, that came from being with him. It was the same warmth that I felt in the presence of my father's friends, older men who it was easy to joke with, men whose shyness in the presence of a young attractive woman somehow rendered them harmless.

Robert's apartment was a small two bedroom with sloping ceilings that sat above a Korean restaurant near campus. It was hard for me to imagine that a man his age, a tenured professor of physics, would live in such a place. The living room was dimly lit and musty, the paint on the walls was stained in places, and there was not much in terms of furniture: several bookcases stocked with old books, a large oak desk, a few finger paintings on the wall. Robert apologized for the size of the place, and the mess, explaining that he had recently separated from his wife and was only renting the apartment temporarily. The finger paintings, he said, were from his daughter.

I pretended to study the paintings with amusement, while Robert took my coat and walked into the kitchen.

"I suppose you want to know," he said, putting the kettle on to boil.

"Know what?" I said.

"Whether you got the equation right."

"No," I said. "I already know I didn't."

"How can you be sure?"

"I just am," I shrugged. "I fucked it up."

He smiled. "Tell me, Heather," he said. "Do you always use that type of language with your professors?"

"No," I said. "Only when they invite me back to their apartments."

He laughed.

"Was I even on the right track?" I asked.

He shook his head. "Honestly," he said. "You weren't even close." Then he smiled. "You know, it took me a year to complete that equation. Dirac himself had trouble reproducing it without notes."

"So what possessed you to give it to us?"

He grinned. "Arrogance is a physicist's greatest hindrance," he said, taking the kettle off the stove and pouring the hot water into a ceramic pot. "As soon as you think you understand something, you eliminate any opportunity for discovery."

"So if I got it wrong," I said. "I mean, if I wasn't right. Why did you invite me here?"

He walked into the room and handed me a tea cup. "Because you were the only one who finished the exam."

I looked at him.

"You were the only one who handed it in," he said. "That was the test. And you passed."

"Do I get an A then?"

"No," he said. "You get some tea."

The rest of the evening we sat in his living room and talked about physics, about Dirac and the origin of the equation, about ourselves. Robert seemed to take a genuine interest in my life—my family and friends, the small town in Connecticut where I had grown up.

And when I spoke to him, I felt a warm rushing in my chest, very different from the type of feverish excitement I felt in the presence of boys my own age. This was a softer, more expansive warmth. I enjoyed the way he asked me questions, candidly, and the way he looked me directly in the eyes when I spoke. He treated me as I imagine he would have treated one of his colleagues, as an adult, an equal. He asked me about my childhood and my parents. He asked me about my early interest in physics and the details of my studies, and before long I found myself relaxing, telling him stories about my mother and how we were in a period of not talking to each other, about how I was not planning to go home for Christmas, and about my ex-boyfriend, Alex Fader, who I once believed I was going to marry, but now could not say more than five words to on the phone. It was warm in his apartment. The insides of his windows were misted up with steam, and he interrupted me only once to turn down the heat and put on a rare recording of Glenn Gould, a tape which he said had been given to him by an old classmate from MIT. As we listened to the tape, Robert explained how so many of his classmates had stopped doing research, how a handful of them taught, like him, and the rest had either taken government jobs or gone into finance. As you get older, he explained, it's easy to become disillusioned by the paradoxes. When you're young, they're a challenge. But when you're old, they simply become frustrating. For all physicists, he said, there is a point when you realize that there is a level of thinking above you—a level you'll never understand. Even the greatest physicists, he said, even Bohr, reached that point. "It's like music," he said. "Talent and practice can take you so far. But very few can do this." He paused to listen to Gould's frenetic playing. Ascending arpeggios, crashing crescendos. "Do you see what I mean?"

I nodded. "That's why you gave us the equation."

"Yes," he said. "That's why I gave you the equation."

"And that's why you invited me here."

"Yes," he said. "I suppose it is."

He smiled weakly, and suddenly in the dim light of his tiny apartment he no longer seemed like the confident lecturer he had been in seminar. Instead, he just seemed like an old man who was a little lonely. He stood up to change the tape, and as he hunched over the stereo I told him in an apologetic voice that I had dinner plans that night. I was sure my friend had long since forgotten me, but I felt a sudden need to avert the imminent awkwardness of the evening. Robert smiled and nodded, and later, as we stood at the door, he helped me with my coat.

"I'd like to see you again sometime, Heather," he said.

I paused for a moment before I stepped into the hallway. "I would like that too," I said.

At that time, I was living in a dorm on the east side of campus. Like a lot of the student population at Brown, the girls on my hall seemed to come from privileged New England families. They cultivated an impoverished activist look, smoked a lot of pot, rarely showered, subsisted on couscous and fava beans, and kept their BMWs well hidden behind the dorm. Almost nightly, they threw loud parties in their rooms, and though I rarely attended these late night gatherings, it was at one of them that I later met my current husband, Colin, who I first began to date less than a month into the following semester. At the time, Colin was finishing up his premed requirements. He was an upperclassman and also somewhat of a celebrity on campus, a swimmer who regularly had his photograph in the campus paper for breaking school records. In retrospect,

Colin was everything that Robert was not—which is to say, he was young and handsome, brazenly opinionated, and filled with a healthy optimism about the world. He wanted to help people, he told me on our first date, and when he said this, in his soft, earnest voice, I believed him.

We were sitting in an Ethiopian restaurant downtown, across the street from the bars where everyone went at night. We had met the previous night at the dorm party, and early the next day he had called to ask me to dinner. Later, he would tell the story differently to our friends. He would claim that it was me who had asked him out, and each time he told it, I was more bold, more smitten with him. But if I had asked him, I don't remember. I had been fairly drunk that night, and the next morning, when he called to remind me of our plans, he had had to say his name several times before I remembered who he was.

As it turned out, I was pleasantly surprised when I saw him that night. He was tall and broad shouldered, bestowed with the freckled skin of someone who had spent his summers in the sun. He was charming in a boyish way, and when I talked to him he smiled and seemed genuinely amazed at the things that came out of my mouth. Over lamb curry and wine, he told me that I was one of the smartest people he had ever met. He said this earnestly—as he said everything—and I blushed and told him that he must not know me very well. Later, as we walked across the street to one of the bars, I let him hold my hand, and afterward, I followed him back to his basement apartment, where we kissed quietly on his couch while his roommate slept soundly down the hall. We were both a little drunk, and eventually Colin fell asleep on my lap. I can still remember how his face looked that evening, how for a long time I just sat there in the darkness of his tiny apartment, touching his hair, not wanting to leave.

Over the next few weeks Colin took me to wrestling meets and hockey games and afterward to small bars around town. I attended his home swim meets ritually and sat in a special section reserved for the swimmers' families and girlfriends. I did not sleep with him during that time, but I would allow him to come to my dorm room each night after his evening practice. Still reeking of chlorine, he would crawl into bed with me, his hair wet and bristly, his skin blotchy in places. He was a sweet person, and still is, but even then he was a rough lover, and when he touched me under my nightgown and pressed his body against me I would brace myself. It was not that I felt uncomfortable with him. It was only that the intensity of his feelings for me scared me. "I think I'm falling in love with you," he would whisper, as he pushed against me, and I would kiss him until he finally stopped talking. Afterward, while Colin slept, I would lift myself on an elbow and watch him. His face always looked so gentle and unassuming at those moments, and I would understand then, in the dim light of my dorm room, that he would one day be the man I married. This is a very different feeling than the feeling you have when you realize you are in love with someone. I wasn't sure if I was in love with him. But as I watched him sleep I understood that I could spend the rest of my life with him. I could raise a family with him and grow old in his company. I could do all of these things, I realized, and not be unhappy.

It was almost a month into the next semester before I heard from Robert again. I had not forgotten about him or our night together in his apartment. But when he called me one night toward the end of the month, I remember being surprised by the sound of his voice. It seemed deeper and softer than I had remembered. It reminded me for a moment of my father's voice, when he used to call me that first year I was away from home.

"I'd like to show you Eisenstein," Robert said.

"Eisenstein," I said. "Is he a physicist?"

"No," he laughed. "A filmmaker."

I was quiet for a moment.

"Do you like films, Heather?"

I told him I did.

"Wonderful," he said. "Then it's a date."

In truth, the decision to meet Robert was not a difficult one. I had been thinking about him since that afternoon in December, and though I did not intend to tell Colin of our meeting, it did not seem like I was doing anything wrong either. I knew that if Colin were to pass Robert and me on the street, he would not think twice about it. It was only in my own mind, and perhaps in my heart, that I understood what I was doing to be a betrayal.

The film Robert took me to see was *The Battleship Potemkin*, a Russian war movie from the 1930s. It was playing at a small bijou near campus, and after dinner I walked into town and met him outside the ticket booth. Afterward, Robert invited me back to his apartment on Durant Street, and gave me some wine and we sat in his kitchen and talked about the film. I hadn't liked it very much and Robert had shook his head and said that this was because I wasn't used to having to work when I went to see a film. Art was something you had to *work* for, he claimed. Still, he smiled and laughed as I critiqued it. I told him how at one point, during one of the battle scenes, I had spotted a Russian cameraman standing in the background of a shot, and how later, in another scene, the resolution had been so poor I'd thought the film had ended. Robert chuckled and shook his head, then stood up and announced that, as of this moment, he was thoroughly disappointed in me. His face was flushed, and it touched me in a way that he trusted me enough to get drunk in my presence. This was only our second time alone together, our first official date, and yet I remember feeling an immediate sense of ease in his presence, a calmness, as if I had known him in some deeper way all my life. And I remember also the secret thrill of sitting next to him in his small kitchen, drinking wine and laughing. We talked late into the night. I don't recall much of what we said. Mostly we talked about physics and his early studies. But I do remember that at one point, after several glasses of wine, Robert suggested that we make a ritual of these evening meetings. He said that we could think of it as a sort of independent study. He would teach me about physics and I would tell him about my life.

"I'm afraid my life's not very interesting," I said.

Robert laughed. "Somehow I find that hard to believe, Heather," he said, leaning over to refill my glass.

"You know, I have a boyfriend," I said.

"I've never assumed otherwise."

"We're serious," I continued. "I mean, we like each other."

Robert smiled. "I'm happy for you."

I looked at him, waiting for something in his face that would suggest his disappointment, but he simply seemed amused.

"Do you know how old I am, Heather?" he asked.

I looked at him.

"I'm probably older than your father."

"That's not what I meant."

"I like talking to you," he continued, as if he had not heard me. "That's all. I enjoy these conversations we have. And I think that you enjoy them too. "

I nodded.

"So?" he said.

"So, when can I see you again?" I asked.

Robert reached into his pocket and slid a key off his key chain, then handed it to me. "Whenever you want," he smiled.

Later that evening, when I returned from Robert's apartment, Colin was waiting in the hallway outside my dorm room. He was wearing his swim team sweat suit and reading a book. When he saw me approaching the door, he stood up and smiled. I could see in his eyes that he was concerned about where I had been, and when he took my hand without a word and kissed me against the wall, I realized the full extent of both his fear and his love for me. I realized that he would have waited all night and that my return had brought him not only relief, but also a sudden conviction of his feelings for me. If he suspected anything, which I assume he must have, he did not say a word. He pressed his face against my neck and eventually I took his hand and led him to my room. Perhaps because he had waited so faithfully for me, or because he had not asked me where I'd been, or because when he squeezed me I realized that I loved him too, as much as I could love any man, I let him make love to me that night. I undressed slowly and lay down next to him on the bed, and as he entered me for the first time, it seemed that I had just opened up a hole in my life—a hole the precise size and shape of Colin—and that nothing in the intricate fabric of my future would ever be the same.

Robert and I made an informal arrangement to meet once a week at his apartment on Durant Street. For a long time we talked purely about physics during these meetings. Each week Robert would tell me a new story about one of his heroes, and each week I would listen. He was earnest when he spoke of Einstein, reverential when he discussed the work of Niels Bohr and Heisenberg. But it was not Robert's stories that I came for. I came because I felt more comfortable in the confines of his small apartment than I'd felt anywhere else in my life. And in the late evenings, as I sat on his couch, I would often wonder whether our friendship would ever move beyond these talks. I didn't know if Robert even wanted that. But sometimes, as we sat together on his couch, I would notice our legs touching, just slightly, or other times, he would reach across the couch and touch my hand as he was telling a story. He'd hold it for a moment, then let go. I knew that he had been an attractive man when he was younger. I had seen pictures of him in his apartment, pictures of him and his wife when they were first married and living in Copenhagen. But it was hard to reconcile the man in the pictures with the man Robert had become. Some evenings, sitting on his couch, I would find myself just watching him, trying to imagine how long it had been since he'd slept with a woman.

As time passed, my meetings with Robert became more frequent, and I began to look forward to them almost as much as I didn't look forward to my evenings with Colin. I began to see Robert once or twice a week in the evenings, while Colin was at work or in the lab writing a paper. If Colin suspected anything, he didn't show it. And if what I was being was unfaithful, I didn't allow myself to believe it. I felt loosened from myself that spring, and in retrospect did not spend much time considering what I was doing. By that time, Robert and I had stopped talking about physics altogether. Instead we had begun to talk about the intimate details of our own lives—past lovers who had betrayed us, past lovers we'd betrayed, moments in our childhood too painful and embarrassing to recall. There was a freedom to these talks, a freedom in the knowledge that whatever was said in that room would never leave that room.

And in this way I was able to talk to Robert about things I could never mention to Colin. I could say anything, however absurd or embarrassing, because it seemed that whatever was said in that apartment would have no bearing on the world outside. Robert would smile as I confessed to fantasies I had had as a young girl, fantasies that involved friends of my father's, teachers at school— always older men. I suppose the impulse had been in me even then, and I imagine that I was trying to tell him something by confessing these crushes. But he did not take advantage of the opportunity, as he probably could have. Instead, he would simply laugh and shake his head at my preadolescent prurience.

"Did you ever love any of them?" he asked me one evening, as we were sitting on his couch. "These men?"

I looked at him. "Are you asking me whether I've ever been in love with an older man?"

"Yes," he said. "I suppose I am."

I paused for a moment, as if considering the question. Then I looked at him and said yes—a yes as deliberate and direct as his question had been.

Robert smiled.

"How about you?" I said. "Have you ever been in love with a younger woman?"

"Oh," he smiled. "I imagine there have been a few." He winked at me. Then he finished his wine and got up to change the record.

That was the closest Robert ever came to flirting with me. I don't think he ever meant for it to go beyond that. After all, this was not the type of flirting that was meant as foreplay. I think he had simply wanted to let me know that he was in love with me, and though a part of me had wanted him to do something at that moment—to grab my hand, or kiss me—I don't think that he ever had the intention of making a move. In fact, I think that Robert felt just as guilty about our involvement as I did. And his ambivalence about taking our friendship to the next level must have come from some deep fear that I'd later resent him for it. I remember one evening, as we were sitting on his couch, telling him a story about my parents' new house. The story was not very interesting, and I could tell after a while that he had stopped listening. When I finally finished, he simply sighed. Then he looked at me sadly and said, "I fear that you'll hate me for this one day, Heather."

"For what?" I said.

"These meetings," he said. "I fear that one day you'll look back on them, and you'll hate me."

I looked at him. "You know what I fear, Robert?" I said, touching his hand. "I fear that I won't."

Alone, walking around campus or sitting in the library stacks, I imagined telling Colin about my meetings with Robert. I imagined what his face would look like and practiced in my mind what I would say. But whatever I came up with seemed inaccurate. It seemed impossible to explain something that I could barely explain to myself. Colin, despite his busy schedule, was a dutiful boyfriend. He took me out to eat once or twice a week, and on the weekends drove us out to Newport, to the coast and the mansions. By then he had begun to hint regularly about our life together after his graduation in May. He would be leaving for medical school, and I would have one more year to go. The choice seemed simple to both of us. I would go with him wherever he went and finish my degree later. We would marry. This was something we had both accepted, but never formally talked about.

"I want to spend the rest of my life with you," Colin said one night, as we were driving home from the coast. It was the first and only time he had ever brought it up.

"I want that too," I assured him.

"You do?"

"Yes."

He smiled. "I'm glad," he said.

Then he touched my hand and I smiled, though it scared me a little, how much he seemed to need me at that moment.

Later that night, lying in bed, I said to him, "You seem so surprised." He was already beginning to talk about the house we would one day own, the names of our kids.

"Not surprised," he said. "Just happy."

That spring I continued to attend Colin's home swim meets regularly, but more often than not, when the team traveled, I would try to beg off, claiming to be exhausted, so I could go see Robert. In the hours after Colin left, I would leave messages on the answering machine at Robert's office, telling him to meet me at his apartment. And later, after letting myself in with the key he had given me, I would sit on his couch alone. Sometimes Robert would never show up, and I would assume that he had gone to have dinner with his wife and daughter. But other nights, he would come home late, long after I had fallen asleep, and he would sit next to me on the couch, quietly, not saying a word, waiting for me to wake.

In technical terms our relationship violated the school's strict non-involvement policy, and Robert often liked to remind me that he could get fired because of me. "I could lose everything because of you," he would say. "If the dean of studies walked through the door right now and found you on my couch, they'd pack me up and send me away." But when he said this, it was always with a smile, as if he took some secret pleasure in this knowledge.

I bring this up now only because it was on a Wednesday, several months after our first meeting, that Robert suggested we go out for a drink. We hadn't been out together since that night at the bijou, and so his suggestion surprised me. I had always thought that he would be afraid of running into one of his colleagues, or his wife, or even one of the other students from our class. But that night Robert simply stood up, lit a cigarette, and said, "I need a drink, Heather. Tonight I need a drink."

"Then, Robert," I said, mimicking his voice. "A drink you shall have."

"Wonderful," he said. "Where should we go?"

"Your choice," I said.

"My choice," he said, smiling. He looked out the window at the late evening sky, darkening in the distance. "Well then," he said. "I know just the place."

The bar we went to was an old pub down the street from Robert's apartment. I had been there once or twice before with Colin and some of his friends. It was a small, dimly lit space with a pool table and a few dartboards against the far wall. Robert said that he liked it because they served a brand of German lager that he used to drink in Copenhagen. But that night we didn't drink beer. We drank Scotch, several glasses each, and it was not until somewhere around the third glass that I leaned across the table and took his hand. I don't know, even now, where the impulse came from. I suppose that I had wanted to let him know that I thought of him in the same way that he thought of me, and though I think that it made him a little uncomfortable, he did not let go. And so we held hands and talked late into the night—about physics, about his wife and their separation, about his early life in Copenhagen—and it was not until sometime later that I looked across the bar and noticed the unmistakable shape of Colin's back, turned away from us. He was not alone. He was with eight or nine guys from the swim team, all in sweats, their hair still wet from evening practice. They were huddled around the television at the far end of the bar, and when I saw them I felt my entire body freeze. And it was at that moment, the moment I first realized what was happening, that Colin turned casually to his friend, glanced over his shoulder, and noticed us. I can still remember the look on his face—part astonishment, part fear. Our eyes met briefly, and then he looked away. Perhaps if I had been sitting across from Robert instead of next to him, or if we had been drinking coffee instead of Scotch, or if I had not been holding his hand, as I was at that moment, Colin would have just walked over and said hi. But instead what he had seen was the two of us sitting together in a booth, half-drunk, holding hands, and it looked bad, which I suddenly realized it was.

It was probably out of some sense of graciousness that Colin did not walk up to us at that moment and make a scene, that he instead remained at the bar, feigning obliviousness and allowing Robert a chance to leave. It seems strange now. But in those brief seconds, I did not even say a word to Robert. He had simply seen it in my face, my expression, the moment I recognized Colin, and he had known the second I let go of his hand that I wanted him to leave. He stood up, smiled, then walked out the door without saying a word. Colin, sitting at the bar, watched him leave, followed him with his eyes as he walked down the street, then a moment later walked over and stood before me. He was waiting for me to say something, waiting for my excuse, but at that moment I didn't have one. Instead, I simply looked down. On the other side of the bar I could hear his teammates, huddled over pitchers of beer, laughing and joking.

"We need to talk," Colin said.

I nodded, without looking at him.

"We need to talk," Colin said again. "Now."

I spent most of the ride home regretting almost everything I had done with Robert and thinking of how I could possibly explain it to Colin. It seemed almost ridiculous that I felt as guilty as I did. After all, there was nothing to hide. It was a friendship, nothing more. But I also knew how it looked. And I knew that Colin would never understand why I had been hiding it from him. As we pulled onto the street where Colin lived, I braced myself for what I thought was coming. But Colin didn't even raise his voice. In fact, he just sat there for a long time, not saying a word. We parked on the street outside his apartment, and as we sat in the car, the heat running, he looked at me seriously and said, "Are you sleeping with him?"

"Jesus Christ, Colin. Of course I'm not sleeping with him."

"I just don't know why you'd lie to me," he said. "Why would you tell me you were going to the movies?"

"I don't know," I said. "I just didn't want you to worry."

"Why would I worry?" Colin asked. "If nothing was going on, why would I worry?"

"I don't know," I said. "Can we please just go inside?"

"How often do you see him?"

"Not often," I lied. "Once in a while. We're friends. Come on, Colin. He's twice my age."

But I could see he wasn't assured.

I was tempted at that moment to tell him the whole thing, to admit to my meetings with Robert and our talks. To tell him that in a way

I loved Robert just as much as I loved him, which I realized, at that moment, was the truth. But I didn't say any of these things. Instead I just kissed him, hoping to kiss it all away, and he pulled back.

"I'm going for a walk," he said.

I nodded and then we both got out of the car and I walked back to my dorm and Colin walked away, in the opposite direction, toward town. I spent most of the night crying, worried that I had forever ruined things with Colin and realizing with some sadness that I would have to end things with Robert. Colin came into my room around two in the morning. He had his own key and he woke me up by tapping on my shoulder. It was dark in the room, but I could see that he was fully dressed and kneeling on the floor beside my bed. He smelled of beer.

"I want you to promise me something," he said.

"Anything," I said.

"I don't care what you've done. I don't even want to know. But I want you to promise me that you'll never see him again."

"I promise," I said.

"You don't have to say that," he said.

"I know I don't," I said.

He nodded. Then he stood up and left. I did not see him again, not for several days. I decided to wait until he called me, until he was ready. And when he did, he was calm and sweet and it was like nothing had ever happened. We never talked about it again and haven't since.

In retrospect, it might seem that I went into a depression after that night, but I think I just became resigned to what my life was slowly becoming. My mother had been a doctor's wife and now, in all likelihood, I too would become a doctor's wife. It had been my greatest fear as a child, but now it no longer scared me. Nor did it excite me. It just seemed inevitable, and when something seems inevitable you can either choose to accept it, or you can be strong and try to fight it. And I wasn't in the right state of mind to be strong. Colin had already been accepted into medical school by then, and I had agreed to go with him to Baltimore in May. The summer after that we would marry. The weeks passed, and it slowly became evident that my life was changing. I realized that from this point on I would probably never have to worry about money again, at least not in the long term. Colin was bright and ambitious and I knew that he would be a great doctor and I, in turn, would have my time free to do whatever I chose. I could work or not work. I could spend my days reading about molecular physics and forming theories that no one would ever know about. I knew, even then, that Colin would expect very little of me, and so, in this way, I began to expect very little of myself.

As it turned out, I did see Robert one more time. I had thought of writing him a letter, but it had been too difficult a letter to write. I wanted to explain it to him in person, so I stopped by his apartment one evening after class. Colin was at swim practice that night and wouldn't be back for several hours, so when I passed by Robert's apartment on my way back from class, I just walked up the stairs and knocked on the door.

Robert smiled when he saw me. He looked tired, overworked, and as I followed him inside and sat down on the couch across from him, I could not bring myself to do the very thing I had come to do. Instead, I just sat there.

After a long silence, Robert took my hand. "You can't see me anymore," he said. "That's what you've come to tell me."

I looked at him.

He nodded. "I understand," he said.

"I'm sorry," I said.

"No need to be."

"I think I might marry him, Robert," I said.

"You think?"

"I am going to marry him," I said.

He nodded and this time he didn't say a word. I had wanted him to show some sign of jealousy. I know now that he had been jealous, but either ignoring the reality of what I was saying or else simply not wanting to believe it, he said, "Are you free tomorrow night?"

"Please Robert," I said. "You're not listening to me."

"I am listening to you," he said. "And I'm asking whether you're free tomorrow night."

I was just then beginning to realize that there was, and would always be, a communication between us that went beyond words. I resented it at the time, how easily he seemed to understand me. He would tell me later that if I had really wanted to end things I would have just called him or written a letter. I wouldn't have come to his apartment in person. But when I had stood on the street outside his apartment that night, I had believed that I did want to end things, and not only because it was the right thing to do, but because it seemed to be what I truly wanted to do. But when he asked me that question and looked at me, it was not out of stubbornness or willful denial that I didn't reply; it was because he seemed to understand me at that moment better than I understood myself.

I handed him the key he had given me, and without saying another word, I hugged him. He leaned down then and I felt him kiss my neck, softly, the first and only time he had ever kissed me.

His lips remained pressed against my skin for several seconds and I did not move until I felt him pull away.

"Thank you," he whispered.

Then I turned around and left and that was the last time I ever saw Robert.

Colin and I married the year after he graduated. He was in medical school then, at Johns Hopkins, and though I hated Baltimore, I tried my best to be what I believed a good wife was supposed to be. I don't mean in the traditional, subservient sense, but in the supportive, understanding sense. I supported us for four years, working as a secretary at a law office, and Colin studied. My memories of that time are pleasant ones, though I know that I have probably romanticized it. For the first three years I kept up a correspondence with Robert from a PO Box in town. We would exchange letters once or twice a month, and though I longed to keep these letters, I would always throw them out as soon as I had read them, fearful of what might happen if I tried to hide them.

The letters Robert and I wrote were not always romantic in nature. In fact, they were more often somewhat banal and ordinary accounts of our daily lives. Several times Robert had hinted about a possible meeting, but I never acknowledged these invitations in my own letters and after a while, he stopped making them. There were also a few occasions when the phone rang late at night and Colin had picked it up and there had been no one on the other end. It could have been anyone, I knew, but for some reason I always felt certain that those phone calls had been from Robert. I had willed myself into believing he was still trying to contact me, though in truth our correspondence tapered off, and after that last summer in Baltimore, stopped altogether.

We moved again for Colin's internship, which was in Coopers-town, New York. As an intern's wife, I was expected to host luncheons and dinners for the other interns' wives. It was somehow required of us. In reality, these luncheons were more like group therapy sessions, during which we would all commiserate about the fact that we never saw our husbands and about how when we did see them they were barely awake. We complained about the shifts, which seemed like some type of military training, and about the long nights alone in our homes. Days would go by when I wouldn't see Colin at all. He often slept on a gurney in between shifts, and called me only to let me know that he wouldn't be coming home. He gained about thirty pounds during that time, living on food from the hospital cafeteria, and his face began to take on a pale, unhealthy hue. I remember one afternoon, watching him in the garden, and being unable to reconcile the image of the man I now saw with the lean and handsome swimmer I had married. We slept together infrequently during that time and I hid from Colin the fact that I was now using birth control. Many of the other interns' wives were already pregnant, and at that time the only thing that seemed worse than going through this period of time alone, was going through it alone and pregnant. Sequestered in our small house by the lake, I watched a lot of television, soap operas and game shows, and set up projects for myself, like reading all of Nabokov's novels, then all of Balzac's. I learned how to play bridge, joined an aerobics group at the YWCA, planted tomatoes in the spring. I thought, but not often, about physics. There was the idea of my unfinished degree, floating over me. At the time, it seemed impossible to imagine that I would ever return to school and finish it.

It was during the second and final year of Colin's internship that I learned of Robert's death. I might never have known of it, in fact, were it not for a dinner party we went to with one of Colin's colleagues, a physics scholar in his youth. Robert had died of lymphatic cancer, his colleague told us that night after dinner, as we were finishing up dessert. I don't know what my face must have looked like upon hearing this news. But I know that I must not have been able to hide my shock and sadness, because Colin excused himself a moment later and went outside to smoke. And later on that night, as we drove home, he did not say a word to me. I realized then that after all these years Colin still thought about that night at the bar—the image of Robert and I holding hands—and in the silence of the car I could now feel a distance, a distance that had been growing between us for years, slowly, in the darkness of our house. That night, I went out in the yard and wailed. I don't know, even now, if Colin heard me.

Colin and I live in San Francisco now. He wanted to take a job with an established group in Boston, but had agreed, after my protests, to finally leave the East. Neither of us had friends or family on the West Coast, but I had always imagined living there one day. As a child I had vacationed there and as the years went by I had managed to convince myself that my depression was seasonal, that it was the bleak and quiet New England winters, as much as anything else, that had sent me into a funk. It is only now that I realize that I wanted to get as far away from Robert and the memory of him as I could. Colin is practicing full time now and we have a house in Walnut Creek. He commutes across the Bay Bridge each morning and I have started taking courses at Berkeley, trying after all these years to finally get my degree. We have begun to try in earnest to have children and I imagine that some day soon we will.

It's naive to assume that another person can fulfill you, or save you, if the two things are, in fact, different, and I have never felt that way with Colin. I simply believe that he fulfills a part of me, an important part of me, and that Robert fulfilled another equally important part of me. The part of me Robert fulfilled is a part which I imagine Colin, even now, doesn't know exists. It is the part of me that can destroy as easily as it loves. It is the part of me that feels safest and most at home behind closed doors, in a dark bedroom, that believes that the only truth lies in the secrets we keep from each other. Robert is the secret that I have kept from Colin for almost ten years. I have imagined telling him sometimes. It has been ten years, and in that time we have lasted through a miscarriage, near bankruptcy, and both of his parents dying, and I feel at this point that there is almost nothing we can't weather together. But it's not that I'm afraid of how he will react. I know him well enough to know that he will internalize it. He may hate me for it, but he would never show me. His whole life, it seems, he has gone out of his way to spare me pain and I know that even as I told him of my feelings for Robert, he would be thinking how not to hurt me. Guilt is the reason we tell our lovers these secrets, these truths. It is a selfish act, after all, and implicit in it is the assumption that we are doing the right thing, that bringing the truth out into the open will somehow alleviate some of the guilt. But it doesn't. The guilt, like any self-inflicted injury, becomes a permanent thing, as real as the act itself. Bringing it out into the open simply makes it everyone's injury. And that is why I never told him. I never told him because I knew he would have never told me.

It is rare these days that I find myself thinking about Robert. I have managed to store the memory of him away in a part of my mind that I reserve only for my most painful and intimate losses. But when I find myself recalling him now, and our brief time together, I return to an evening shortly before things ended with us. It was an evening in early spring, an unseasonably cold night when

Colin had gone off with some of his friends to a post-tournament party. I had begged off, claiming that I was sick, and then, as soon as Colin had left, I had walked over to Robert's apartment and let myself in with the key he had given me. It was not the first time I had let myself in with this key, but it was the first time I had gone over to his apartment with the intention of making love to him.

I knew that Robert had an evening class that night and that he'd be back some time before nine. And so I drank some wine to give myself courage and then undressed and lay under the sheets on his bed. I had the image of him coming in and finding me there, the sheet covering my body, my bare shoulders exposed. I planned in my mind what I would say when he came in from the cold and discovered me. Maybe, I decided, I would not say a thing. I tried to imagine Robert's expression. I wondered if he would turn his head, but hoped he wouldn't. It was a gift that I was giving him and I hoped that he would understand that.

In the end, I lay in his bed for almost two hours. The room was lit only by Robert's desk lamp in the corner, and after a while the room grew dark and I realized that he would not be coming back. I realized that he had probably gone to his wife's house to have dinner and that he would probably spend the night there as well. Slowly, I sat up in his bed and got dressed, knowing that I would never do anything like this again. But before I left, I poured myself a glass of wine and smoked a cigarette and sat at the table, watching the students out on the street, tossing a football in the snow. They were my age, but at that moment they seemed so much younger than me. And it was a strange moment, sitting there in the dark, drinking Robert's wine, realizing that eventually, maybe not for a few hours, but eventually, I would have to leave.

river dog

IT IS EASY NOW, after everything that has happened to my
brother, to say I didn't hate him. But I can still remember how it
used to humiliate me when the rumors about him spread through
my high school. How he once killed a stray cat with a hockey stick,
or another time, how he jumped out of a third-story window of the
school on a dare. On bus rides home from field trips, I'd pretend
to be asleep while the stories about him began to circulate. Someone would claim to have heard Doug having sex with a dog in the
cornfield behind our school. Someone else would swear they'd seen
him sleeping in their yard. I'd close my eyes, turn up my Walkman,
and pretend it was someone else, not my brother, they were talking
about.

Doug had graduated from my high school four years before, but
the stories about him remained, were passed down from year to

year like a tradition. He was still living in my parents' house at the time, working various jobs at the mall, none of which ever lasted long. Most of the time it seemed he was in between jobs, living off whatever money my parents gave him. He slept in a small, damp room in our basement, and when he wasn't working spent his days hanging around my high school. *Not right* was the term people used for him. He was not right, the way he still dated high school girls, the way he didn't hold down a job, the way he showed up at school some days just to see me and say hi. I would see him lurking in the hallway sometimes. He'd be talking to his girlfriend—a senior named Michelle—and behind his back, people would laugh. They'd tell him to get a job. They'd sing "Desperado." And sometimes, if they pushed hard enough, he'd try to fight them. Other times I'd just hear about it. Someone would claim to have heard Doug whistling in the hallway during seventh period. Someone else would swear they'd seen him in his poncho, wandering around the parking lot, looking through classroom windows, grinning.

In the evenings after school, Doug hung around the athletic fields and watched Michelle's field hockey practice. Sometimes his friend Trey, who was around the same age, would stop by too. They would smoke cigarettes and watch from the top bleacher and eventually someone, a kid from the junior high, would walk up and ask Doug if he could score him some dope. If I was there, Doug would shake his head, tell the kid to go away. He'd say, "I don't know what you're talking about, friend. I don't do that."

But it always embarrassed me. It always made me feel a sudden and urgent need to be elsewhere. By the time I was seventeen it seemed my brother had ruined whatever social potential I once believed I had. He made it impossible for me to be anything more than what I was already, which was invisible. People even forgot sometimes that we were brothers. In the locker room after gym class, guys would talk about him, forgetting I was in earshot. They'd say, *That guy is just completely fucked in the head.*

The summer I turned seventeen was Doug's last at home. It was a humid summer, full of cloudy and quiet afternoons. Most days Doug and I looked for ways to stay out of the heat, smoking cigarettes and listening to records down in the damp basement of our house, where his bedroom was. And in the cool of each evening, I sat on the back porch and studied for the SATs, while Doug worked on our father's 1963 Harley Super Glide in the backyard. In the sixties our father had taken this bike cross-country, and now it was Doug's—one of the few presents I could remember my father giving him. Doug's goal was to get the bike all cherried up and running by August so that he could ride it down to the docks in Norfolk, Virginia, and make a big impression. Earlier that year he had committed to a job on a petroleum rig after our father had threatened to kick him out of the house, and now, almost six months later, he was still too stubborn to admit it had been a mistake.

"I figure, I make it through the first week, I'm fine," Doug said one night, as we were working on the bike. "That's when they really beat the shit out of you."

"People die on those rigs," I said.

He shrugged as if death was not a consequence that concerned him.

"You're counting the days, I guess."

"I don't know," I said.

Doug crouched down beside the bike and I passed him tools as he pointed to them.

"Maybe I'll join you next year," I said.

"I wouldn't," he said. "Not if you can help it." He straightened

the front wheel with his hand. "Not if you have another option."
Then he started to smile in a strange way.

"Michelle and I are getting married," he said.

"Oh yeah?"

"I haven't asked her yet, but I'm basically sure she'll say yes."

I nodded.

"You don't believe me?"

"No," I said, "I believe you."

Michelle was a senior who I had sat next to in Biology that past spring. Doug dated her off and on, and there was a rumor that he had once gotten her pregnant and that she'd had an abortion. I knew that she cared about Doug, and I sometimes even believed that she loved him, but she was leaving for college that next fall and I doubted she'd ever marry him.

During Biology class, Michelle and I had passed notes, and nights she was out with Doug I had let her copy my homework, but most of what I knew of her was from what Doug had written in the spiral notebook he kept hidden under his mattress. He wrote a lot about wanting to marry her, despite the fact she was five years younger than him. And he wrote a lot about the house he planned to buy for them, the names of their kids. Sometimes there were long passages almost resembling poems and occasionally I'd find a page where he had drawn a picture of a sultry woman, usually naked, and underneath it, written her name.

Evenings, when Doug wasn't working on the bike, Michelle would come pick him up in her Volvo. Usually they'd go to parties on the other side of town, in Clearview or Eschelman Heights, or one of the other neighborhoods where Michelle and all the other college-bound students lived. Other nights they'd just drive out to the country with Trey and some girl, and occasionally they'd even ask me to come along. If Trey was going, I'd say no. For Trey, my only function was to make him look good in front of his date, to sit there while he called me a pussy and a faggot and asked me when I was finally going to get laid.

But I always had a good time when it was just Doug and Michelle. On nights when there wasn't a party, we'd head straight out to the deep country, past the Amish farms, and park on some cliff overlooking the Conestoga River and the whole county. There'd be a cool breeze coming up off the water, the sun descending beyond the fields, and we'd get drunk on a case of Hamm's or Olympia. Eventually Doug would stand up, stretch, and say, "Okay little man. Be back in a second." Then I'd wait while he and Michelle went into her Volvo and screwed.

I never minded. And it never occurred to me that my brother was a grown man, almost twenty-three, or that what he was doing was *not right*. When they came back from the car, Doug would give me a smile behind Michelle's back. Then we'd all throw stones into the river below us for good luck.

The first time I actually heard the story about Carrie Huber was from Trey, who told it like a joke. Carrie Huber had outdone herself, he said one night in late July while we were waiting in the car for Doug. Trey was laughing as he told me the story. He and Doug both, he said, out behind the pool house at Jennifer Benson's Fourth of July party in the Heights. Trey tried to make it seem funny somehow, a conquest on their part, and for Carrie, a drunken blunder, the kind you shake your head at the next morning while you nurse your hangover. *Did I really do that?*

Later, there were other versions of the story. Versions I heard at various parties that summer. In one version Doug and Trey lead Carrie up into the hills behind the Bensons' and hold her down against a large rock, leaving bruises on her tailbone the next day. In another, they slip her a Dramamine to knock her out and afterward shave her pubic hair. Sometimes I pretended to listen to these stories, feigning surprise, as if I had not been there, waiting in the kitchen the whole time. *No shit, they just completely lost it*, someone would say. And I would almost want to correct them, those moments when the story got too wild.

When I think about that night now, it's mostly in terms of images. I'll imagine Doug's expression afterward, coming back into the kitchen from the Bensons' backyard. In my memory he is all smiles, though his smile is doing something funny. He is blinking, sweating. He tells me he wants to leave the party "pronto" and I try to get him to stay. I pour him a drink, try to calm him down, but he is already out the door, crossing the Bensons' lawn. Then I'm following him to the car. He slams the door. "So what happened?" I ask as we turn on Centerville Road, speeding down the dark streets toward the other side of town where we live. "Nothing," he says. "What do you mean?" And I want to say what I mean, I want to say exactly what I mean, but instead I just say, "I don't mean anything." Then we are home again, and for once our father is not asleep in front of the TV, so we turn it on. It is our favorite: *The Creature Double Feature* on channel 2. We sit silently, not looking at each other, and watch.

There was a small dump not far from our house. As kids, Doug and I would look for dead animals there, people's pets that were just dumped off, or else river dogs—one from a group of strays that lived in the tall grass down by the river. When I was in junior high, we went there almost every day, like a ritual. Sometimes one of the dead dogs would still have its collar on and Doug would lean down to check its name. "Sam," Doug would announce. "Sam is dead."

Down behind the dump was the Pequea River. In April and May when it flooded out, when the rains came, people would drift down on black inner tubes with coolers of beer strapped in between. Occasionally we'd see a whole group of these people completely naked, even the women, sunning themselves as they drifted downriver.

I remember one afternoon in mid-July, our first summer in Pennsylvania, we spotted two women in the distance, waving at us. They were tan and beautiful. They were in with a large group of men with baseball caps and mirrored sunglasses. Probably they had come down from Hershey or some place north of us. They were drinking. And as they drifted by, the two women started whistling at us, asking us to come on in, the water was nice and cool, and so on. They even pulled up their skimpy black T-shirts a few times, flashing us their tiny white breasts. All the men were laughing and applauding.

Eventually, one of the women peeled her T-shirt off completely and tossed it into the water. Doug was already stripped down to his cutoffs by then. His face was shining.

"Come on," he was saying to me. "Let's go."

"No. No way," I said.

"Come on, little man. She wants you."

I shook my head.

"Okay," he said. "Whatever." Then he did a sort of sideways dive into the muddy water and swam after them.

Even at the time, I realized it was a bonehead move. Before Doug had even reached midriver, two of the larger guys jumped off their tubes and grabbed ahold of him. One of the guys, a bearded man, held Doug's arms back, while the other shoved his head under water. The two women continued to reach for him. *Come here, honey*, they were laughing. I watched as Doug's legs kicked desperately at the air. The more he struggled, the more the others howled. I honestly believed they were going to kill him. I started screaming, telling them to lay the fuck off or I'd call the cops. This went on for about ten minutes.

When Doug finally swam back, he was coughing up water.

"You okay?" I asked.

He nodded. "Complete assholes," he said. "Complete fucking assholes."

Then he turned his back to me and started getting dressed. And it was then, as he was putting on his clothes, that I realized he was crying, and the sight of my brother—six feet tall and thick chested—stooped over, crying, scared me. For a moment, I almost felt sorry for him, almost forgave him for all the times he had beaten me up, all the times he had humiliated me. I said something to him then, I don't remember, and he ignored me. We walked home in silence, and never talked about it again.

When I was in college, I tried to write an essay about what had happened that night at the Bensons' party. My professor handed the essay back to me a week later and said I needed to revise it. At the top of the paper, she wrote: "The reader deserves to know what really happened."

Lying in bed at night, I used to try to construct it in my mind from what I knew:

It is late, one or two in the morning, and Carrie Huber has walked out into the backyard, maybe in search of a cool breeze, a respite from the stagnant summer heat. She is feeling sick from drinking so much, and when Trey finds her, she is vomiting into the rhododendron bushes behind the pool. He watches her for a moment, then heads back to the party. Later, when he returns with Doug, she is passed out. It is like she is asleep, and they try to shake her awake, maybe even try talking to her. They are behind the pool house, out of sight of the party, and they talk about it for a while. Maybe they even decide that it would be what she'd want to do if she were awake. She is not a virgin, after all. She is rumored to have been with half the soccer team. They laugh about it for a while. Then, there is no more talking. One of them, maybe Doug, presses her shoulders to the ground while the other slips off her shorts, unbuttons her blouse.

I imagine Carrie Huber waking up hours later in the Bensons' backyard, naked, wondering what has happened, and then realizing it. I imagine her standing up, getting dressed and moving slowly out of the darkness of the yard, back toward the party, toward the bright fluorescent light of the kitchen, where everyone is giggling. They are nudging her, winking. *So where have you been all night? Say, why's your blouse so wrinkled?* That type of thing, and Carrie smiling.

"Really. Come on. Fuck you," she might say, trying to be herself, which is a little sarcastic, a little crass—but also realizing somehow that she doesn't really know what has happened. Maybe she doesn't even think about it until the next morning, waking up on the Bensons' couch, finding her shorts soiled, blouse torn, noticing that she is sore: a cramp that is not sharp, but duller and deeper.

Earlier that evening, the evening of the party, we had started out drinking by the Conestoga River. It was Doug, Michelle, Trey, and me. We brought a hibachi and had a kind of cookout by the water. The sun was strong. The world seemed clarified. Families were there with plaid blankets and dogs, thick lines of blue smoke bleeding from their barbecues.

The river was where everyone went on the Fourth of July to shoot off fireworks. It was the only place legal if you owned any serious fireworks. Our intentions were to stay all night, watch the show, listen to the Doors, and get drunk. In some ways it was one of the best Fourth of Julys. It was one of the few times that we all got along. Trey, in his own indirect way, was even friendly with me, opening my beers, offering me drags off his cigarette. Doug got sentimental at one point and put his arm around me.

"I love you, little man," he kept saying. "Honestly. I mean it."

At one point Doug and Michelle wandered over to the water by themselves. Trey and I sat on the blanket and watched a group of Boy Scouts shoot off pathetic bottle rockets into the river. I don't know what Doug and Michelle said to each other. Doug stood there hugging himself, while Michelle talked. After a while Michelle started walking in the opposite direction from us, up toward a group of sophomores from my high school, and we didn't see her again that night.

A few minutes later Doug came back and said he wanted to leave.

"Jesus," he said. "Motherfucker."

Trey and I didn't press. Doug and Michelle broke up every other week practically, and none of this seemed unusual. At one point Trey decided that the thing to do now was crash the party over at the Bensons' house.

"Maybe Michelle will show up later," he said to Doug. "Maybe we'll all get lucky."

Doug nodded. "Right," he said. "Okay."

On the ride over, Doug explained how he had asked Michelle to marry him a few days before and how she had turned down his proposal. It was a long, complicated story and I could see his face growing more and more agitated as he told it. When he finished, he explained that earlier that afternoon he had asked her again, and once again she'd said no. According to Doug, she had gotten her mind set on going to Westminster College in the fall, and was no longer interested in going down to Virginia with him. He mimicked her voice as he talked. Finally, he said that a few minutes ago, after a lot of consideration, he had given her one last chance to say yes, down by the river.

I started laughing. Then Trey did, too. Trey said, "You fucking asked her three times?"

The Bensons owned a beautiful white colonial in the northern section of Eschelman Heights. Their house was surrounded by wooded hills and there was a pool and tennis court in the back. They had one of the few lawns in the county that didn't turn yellow during the drought season each July.

That first summer we lived in Pennsylvania Doug and I used to pass it on our bikes. We used to go there all the time, pretending it was our neighborhood. We'd pass the Bensons', the Hubers', the Fultons'. Sometimes they would have parties on their front lawns with big tents and a line of about fifty cars parked down the street. We'd walk right in, take food off the buffet table, smoke cigarette butts out of the ashtrays, drink the half-finished gin and tonics people left at their tables. No one ever noticed us. They never once even asked who we were.

When we arrived at the Bensons' that night there was a group of grown-ups in the kitchen drinking bourbon. In the middle of the kitchen was a keg of beer and a stack of plastic cups. Out on the back lawn, near the pool, a group of girls, including Carrie, stood around a bowl of spiked Hawaiian Punch. Doug, Trey and I stood next to a small record player in the corner of the kitchen and held our beers. No one noticed us. From time to time, one of the grown-ups, jingling ice in a glass, would come over and ask us where we planned on going to college.

Trey would smirk. "Yale," he'd say. "Yale or Princeton. I'm torn."

The grown-ups would always smile at this, sometimes nod in approval, then disappear slowly into the other room. At one point, an older man put his arm around Trey and said that there was someone he wanted to introduce him to, and they walked out to the yard. Doug shook his head.

"Having fun?" he asked.

I nodded.

"Good," he said. "I'm glad to hear it." Then he turned toward the window, stared at the backyard, and downed the rest of his beer.

Most of what happened after that is a blur:

I get very drunk that night, drunk enough that I don't feel self-conscious or embarrassed that I'm with my brother and Trey. Around ten, the grown-ups leave, and the party grows. People start showing up with cases of beer and champagne. Kyle Glass, a senior from my high school, stands and talks to me in the kitchen. He has never spoken to me before, does not in fact know who I am, but in the drunken haze of the party, he suddenly seems interested in me. He wants to know if I'm planning on going out for the soccer team that next fall. I lie and tell him I'm thinking about it.

"Good," he says. "Excellent."

Later on, Carrie Huber and a bunch of her friends come into the kitchen and start talking to me and Kyle. I am drunk and actually feeling somewhat confident talking to them. Carrie starts telling us about her recent trip to Ocean City. She is already drunk, and some of the guys are trying to put their arms around her. She smiles, laughs, pushes them away. Then there is a shout from the living room, and we all head out to watch. One of the boys from Clearview is being stripped. It has become a ritual at parties this summer for people to get stripped. It happens if you pass out. It's mostly the guys who get stripped, then the girls are called in to rate them. Most of the girls will close their eyes, say *Oh God, gross*, then rush out of the room. But there are some girls, like Carrie, who go along with it, who laugh or make a joke, before turning around and heading out the door. It is a game, the whole thing, and though it is rare that one of the girls is actually stripped, there are rules for when it happens. *Only down to her underwear*, one of the boys will yell. *No further.*

Some time later that night, around one, people start setting off fireworks in the backyard. Everyone heads out to watch. Doug and I stay in the kitchen and talk. He seems to be in good spirits again, no longer thinking about Michelle. We stand by ourselves in the corner, drinking from the keg, and I start telling him about the designs I have on various girls at the party. He nods and says, "Good luck, little man." A little later Trey comes in from the backyard, through the Bensons' sliding screen door, laughing, saying that he has found Carrie Huber passed out cold behind the Bensons' pool house.

"You won't believe it," he says to Doug. "You've got to see this."

Everything you would expect to happen afterward didn't. There were no phone calls made to parents, no talk of Carrie Huber pressing charges or getting the police involved. Nothing like that. In fact, the story only circulated in a limited way among the kids from my high school, though it became more distorted and disturbing as the summer progressed.

In the evenings, Doug and Trey continued to go down to the river and get drunk. And once in a while Michelle would stop by our house to see Doug. They would stand out on the edge of our front lawn and talk, and sometimes laugh, lightly.

I stayed at home by myself almost every night or else I rode my bike down to the river and looked for river dogs. I worried sometimes on my rides down to the river that some of the kids from my high school would spot me and say something about Doug. The few times anyone had asked me about it, I had found myself telling them that the whole story was bullshit, exaggeration.

By the end of the summer, I was hardly talking to Doug anymore. I avoided him. I stayed up in my room with the door locked. The closest we ever came to talking about that night was a week or so before he left for Virginia. I was sitting out on the back porch reading, while Doug worked on the Harley. After a while, he came over and started talking about the bike. I wouldn't look at him as he spoke and finally he stopped and said, "I guess you think I'm crazy."

"I don't know what to think," I said.

"Would you believe it if I said I didn't feel like myself that night?"

"I don't know," I said. "I don't know what I'd believe."

He nodded. There was a long silence. Then he said, "I'm an asshole, right?"

"Right," I said.

Doug scraped the mud off his boot. "I guess I don't have anything else to say to you," he said. "I had a lot to say before, but I guess I forgot it."

I stood up. "Well maybe you'll remember it later," I said, and then I walked back inside.

There wasn't a particular day when people stopped talking about that night, just as there wasn't a particular day when the rumor started. It just went away. People forgot. That next fall nothing seemed unusual. Nothing changed. I hadn't had many friends the year before, and I still didn't have many friends. I went to school, tried out for the soccer team, sat on the bench all season, got a scholarship to Penn State, and was on my way up to State College, Pennsylvania, the next fall. After a while no one even talked about what had happened that Fourth of July, just like no one ever talked about how Eric Levengood had driven his car into a highway median the summer before and died. By September, it was old news.

Sometimes when I think about Carrie now, I wonder what she must think about. I wonder if she ever comes home anymore, or if she has forgotten our whole sleeping town. I wonder how long it was before she had a boyfriend again, how long it took her to get over that night and move on with her life. I never knew her, never even spoke to her, but I have thought more than once about writing her a letter, asking her what really happened.

As far as I know, she never talked about it to anyone. She stopped going to parties after that night and left for college some time in August. Once, a few years later, I saw her at a Christmas party. Her hair was short and she was laughing, and I almost wanted to say something to her. I felt like I had a lot to say. But she only stayed a few minutes, exchanged some greetings with her friends, then left. I wondered, even then, if she knew who I was.

In late August, right before Doug left for Virginia, he gave me our father's 1963 Harley Super Glide. He had spent the better part of that morning polishing it up, stitching up the leather seat and rubbing down the chrome. Around noon, he called me outside. "Here," he said. "For putting up with me all these years."

"I don't know how to drive it," I said.

He shrugged. "You'll figure it out." Then he touched me on the shoulder. "Are we straight?"

I nodded.

He patted me on the shoulder again. "Okay, little man," he said. "Take care of yourself."

Later that day our father drove him to the bus station and my mother cried. I took the Harley out on the road and drove it around until it was dark out and my arms felt like rubber. Six months later, on an icy morning in January, I'd take that same motorcycle into a bad spill, break my arm, and never ride it again. In college, a friend of mine would take a similar spill and die, going forty-five miles an hour on a rain-slick road in Unionville, Pennsylvania. I am twenty-six years old now and I can already count on both hands the people I've loved who have died. Doug is not one of them. He refinishes boats now, down in Charleston. We don't talk much anymore.

And I've never told this story to anyone before. But sometimes, when my girlfriend asks, I'll tell her about that first summer we lived in Pennsylvania when I was thirteen and Doug came home drunk one night with a bunch of his friends and tossed a piece of limestone brick through the passenger window of our neighbor's Pontiac. I explain how I was sitting out on the porch and watched the whole thing in disbelief. The next day our neighbor Mr. Kahler came over and accused Doug of smashing the window, said his wife had even seen him do it. Doug denied everything and then there was a big argument. They went at it, Doug and Mr. Kahler, for about twenty minutes. Finally, my mother apologized and wrote Mr. Kahler a check.

I tell my girlfriend that later, after Mr. Kahler left, I went out and started sweeping up the shattered glass on the street, brushing it off the vinyl car seat of his Pontiac. The limestone brick was still lying on the floor of the car.

A few minutes later, Mr. Kahler came out of his house and told me I didn't have to do that. He said—and this is what always gets me—he said, "This has nothing to do with you son."

departure

THAT SPRING WE WERE SIXTEEN Tanner and I started dating the
Amish girls out on the rural highway—sometimes two or three at
the same time, because it wasn't really dating. There was no way
of getting serious.

This was in 1992, over ten years ago, and things had not yet begun to change in our part of Pennsylvania. I think of that year as
a significant one now, a turning point in our county, the first year
the town of Leola started growing and becoming a city and also
the first year the Amish started leaving, selling their property and
heading west toward Indiana and Iowa.

There had been several cases of runaways among the Amish
that year—mostly young men, barely in their twenties, tempted by

the shopping malls and bars popping up along the highways near their farms. Leola was expanding quickly then, it was becoming more common, and it worried the elders in the Amish community. And I think it explains why that spring some of the Amish teenagers were given permission to leave their farms for a few hours on Friday nights.

Out on the other side of town there was an intersection on the rural highway where they would go to hang out. It was a remote area. A strip mall with a Kmart sat on one side of the intersection and across the road there was a twenty-four-hour diner. You would sometimes see them on Friday evenings traveling in a long line like a funeral procession, their buggies hugging the shoulder of the road as tractor-trailers rubbered by. They would park out of sight behind the Kmart, tie their horses to lampposts or the sides of dumpsters, and then the younger ones would go into the Kmart to play video games and the older and more adventurous would cross the street to the diner.

The diner was a family-style place, frequented only by local farming families and truckers, and it was usually empty. Inside, the Amish kids would immediately disappear into the bathrooms and change into blue jeans and T-shirts that they had bought at Kmart, clothes which never seemed to fit their bodies right. Then they would come out, their black wool clothes stuffed into paper bags, and order large platters of fried food and play country songs on the jukeboxes, and try to pretend they weren't Amish.

That spring Tanner and I had begun stopping by just to see them. We never bothered them, just watched. And it never occurred to us that there might be something unnatural about what we were doing, or even wrong. We were simply curious. We wanted to know if the rumors we had heard in school were true: that there were spectacular deformities to be found among the Amish, that few of the children possessed the correct number of fingers, the results of extensive inbreeding.

We would sit in a booth at the far end of the diner and glance at them from behind our menus. We were amazed to hear them curse and see them smoke cigarettes. Some of them even held hands and kissed. Sometimes other people, people from town like us, would stop by, just to watch—and you could tell that it worried them. People were still scared of the Amish then, they were still a mystery and a threat because of their wealth and the tremendous amount of land they owned—and so naturally they were disliked, treated as outsiders and freaks.

At eleven o'clock, they'd change back into their clothes and very politely pay their checks. Then they'd cross the street in a big group, climb back into their buggies and leave. And Tanner and I would stand out in the diner parking lot and watch them, still not believing what we had seen, but also somehow sad to see them go.

Once the other kids at school found out about the diner, they started coming regularly in their Jeeps and BMWs—not to watch like Tanner and I, but to mock and torment. It was cruel and it saddened us to see, though we never once tried to stop it. Instead we sat back in the corner and watched, angry, but also privately relieved that for once it was not us who were being teased or beat up. In the midst of targets so uncool and vulnerable as Amish teenagers, the popular kids seemed to have practically forgotten us.

There was one Amish kid who looked older than the rest. He could have been in his twenties. Tanner and I had noticed him the very first night because of his size and because of his face which always looked angry. He came every week with the rest of them, but always sat off by himself in a separate booth, smoking cigarettes and punching heavy metal songs into the jukebox at his table.

His anger scared us more than the others. That and his size. He had the body of a full-grown man, a laborer—his shoulders broad, forearms solid and bulging out near his elbows.

When the fights started he was always involved. They usually happened out by the dumpsters in back of the diner. The odds were never even: always five or six against one. Having been raised strict pacifists, almost none of the Amish would fight. But he would. And despite his size he would, of course, always lose—though he'd last longer than anyone would believe, moving with the grace of a young boxer, gliding, ducking. His style was to stay low and bring his punches up from way down under. He was quick, had a powerful jab, and knew how to protect himself. But the beauty of his moves never lasted long. Inevitably he'd lose his focus, turn his back or look away for a second, and there would be a pile-on.

A few minutes later, his face cut up and swollen, he'd retreat across the street to Kmart, followed by the rest of the Amish teenagers. And the next week, to everyone's surprise, he'd be back again—not even bitter about it, just sitting there at the edge of the booth, waiting.

It wasn't until late April that Tanner and I started dating the girls, but like I said, it wasn't really dating. They were all extremely shy and there wasn't a whole lot of common ground. Mostly we would ask them questions about their lives, and they would nod or shake their heads and giggle, and then we would sit and watch as they nervously stuffed their faces with cheeseburgers.

Later, we would walk them back across the street to Kmart, and then sometimes, if no one else was around, they would kiss us in the shadows. And then—almost like it never happened—they'd be gone again and we'd have to wait a whole week. Sometimes they'd never come back, and we wouldn't know why. We couldn't exactly call them up. Usually we didn't even know their names. So if they didn't show the next week, we'd try to meet two new ones.

Back at our school, pretty girls wouldn't look at us. We were unexceptional—failures at sports and our fathers didn't manage banks or practice orthopedic medicine. But out on the rural highway we dated the most beautiful of the Amish girls. They were attracted to our foreignness; and we, to theirs.

At school, there were jokes about us, naturally. Mainly inbreeding jokes. Someone had heard that our girlfriends had two heads, three nostrils, tails coming out of their backbones. It was almost summer and so we tried to ignore it, ride it out, though it made us think about what we were doing.

And it was not right, what we were doing. We were aware of that. And in a way we were still scared of the Amish. Even the girls. There was something unnatural about them. It's hard to explain, but they would only let you get so close—and it was always in private where no one else could see. Sometimes they would kiss you and then run away, or else you would be thinking about making a move, not even doing anything, and they would start to cry for no reason, like they knew.

I wonder now if it wasn't worse to let them leave the farms only once a week—if giving them only a small taste of freedom did not make the temptation stronger. Perhaps that's why so many never came back: it was simply too hard.

Tanner came from country people, though he had grown up in town like me. It didn't seem to make a difference. The wealthy kids still called him a hick and made fun of the way he talked and dressed. And you did not want to have the stigma of being from the country in our high school. Tanner and I both lived on the edge of the wealthy area, just across the street from it really. We were in the seventh grade when the school zone switched and the school district agreed to let us finish out our education at Cedar Crest High where all the beautiful and wealthy kids went, the only decent school in the county.

I had grown up with them, the wealthy kids, and even sometimes felt aligned with them when I'd see some of the dirty and disreputable country kids raising hell at our dances. But among them, sitting in class or walking in the hall, I was aware of our differences. Up until the ninth grade I had lied about my father's occupation, told people that he did a lot of work overseas, that his job was sort of secretive and I was not at liberty to discuss it. College wrestling coach didn't sound that great next to heart surgeon or judge. But I don't think anyone believed me anyway. They knew where I lived and knew that I was not a member of the country club, and that I was friends with Tanner. We were not one of them, Tanner and I, though we were not as low as country people either.

There was one girl I saw consistently that summer. Her name was Rachel. She wasn't shy or afraid of the outside world. And her hair smelled like tall field grass, a sweet smell. She was beautiful, too. She did not look like the other Amish girls; she lacked the full-bodied German figure, the solid thighs, the broad shoulders, the round doughy face. She was thin, small framed and with different clothes could have easily passed for one of the popular girls at Cedar Crest.

She was curious, too. Some nights she would want to leave the diner and ride around in Tanner's truck. She would beg Tanner and me to take her into town. Or else she would want to drive out to the Leisure Lanes bowling alley to shoot pool and smoke cigarettes. She was always excited, anxious, wanting to do and see as much as possible in the few hours she had.

When we were alone, Rachel wanted to know everything about me. She wanted to know what my school was like, what my house was like, what it was like to go to Ocean City. She wanted it all described to her in detail, almost like she was saving it up, collecting it.

Only once when we were parked outside the diner did she tell me about her family. It was an enormous family, she said. More than twenty of them lived in one house. Her father was seventy years old, the patriarch of the entire household, and he had set up rules and standards based on the very first order of Amish, now three hundred years old. These were standards that she was expected to uphold and pass down to her children. She had an obligation, she said, being one of the chosen very, very few. But she seemed upset as she told me these things. I could tell it made her feel guilty to think about her family, especially when we were together. And after that one night we never talked about them again.

All summer the heat was getting worse. It had not rained for a record six weeks. Out in the deep country the crops were drying up and in town the grass on people's lawns, even in the wealthy areas, was turning into a yellow thatch. There was no escaping it. Even at night the air was thick with humidity and stuck to your skin like wet towels.

One thing Rachel liked to do was go down to the river valley where there was an old railroad track that had been out of service for more than fifty years. In all that time no one had ever thought to take down the tracks. They were rusted now, covered with weeds, and you could follow them for a mile or so to where they crossed over the river on an old wooden bridge, more than thirty feet high.

Rachel liked to have barefooted races across the planks of the bridge. The planks were evenly spaced, about two feet apart from each other. With a full moon it was easy, you could see where you were stepping, but other nights it would be pitch black and you would have to do it blind. It came down to faith. That and timing. If you slipped once, if your timing was just slightly off, your foot would slide into an empty space and you might snap a shin bone, or worse, if you were unfortunate and slipped through, you might fall thirty feet into the water. And of course we were young and confident and so we never once slipped, or fell, or even stumbled. The trick was always to get a rhythm in your head and to concentrate on it. But like I said, it mainly came down to faith, an almost blind trust that the wooden plank would be right there when you put your foot down. And it always was.

Tanner would sometimes come along with a girl he had met that night and we would all take a blanket and some iced tea down by the river and sit out underneath the stars. Some nights it was so hot Tanner and I would take all our clothes off and jump in the water, and the girls would watch us and giggle, never once thinking to join us; and we, of course, never asked. We knew the limits. We knew how far to push things and the truth was we never wanted to push, being inexperienced in those matters ourselves, and also not wanting to ruin what we had. We were young and somehow sex seemed intricately entwined with those other things—responsibility and growing up—and we were not interested in anything like that.

By then we had stopped hanging out at the diner altogether.

It was no longer exciting to watch the fights and Rachel said it depressed her. More and more people had started coming out to watch the boy who always fought, and he was becoming a bit of a local celebrity. Rachel told me one night that she knew him. She said that his name was Isaac King and that she'd gone to school with him up until the third grade when his parents pulled him out to work. She said that during that past winter he had watched his brother die in an ice-skating accident and that everyone thought he had gone a little crazy from it. He had stopped going to church, she said, and it was only a matter of time before he left the community altogether.

Some Fridays we'd just drive, the three of us, with Rachel sitting between Tanner and me. Tanner liked to take his father's truck onto the backcountry roads that were all dirt and race it with the headlights off. It was terrifying and more fun than almost anything I've ever done—coming around those narrow curves at a high speed, not knowing what to expect, sometimes not even knowing if we were on the road or not, and then flying a little, catching some air when there was a bump or a small hill. Rachel loved it the most, I think. She'd close her eyes and laugh and sometimes even scream—she was not afraid to show her fear like Tanner and me—and finally, when she was on the verge of tears, she would beg Tanner to stop.

"No more!" she would scream. "Pull over!" And he would.

By July everything was changing quickly. Many of the Amish were already leaving, selling their farms to the contractors who had harassed them for years. Rachel never talked about it much, though I know that it was on her mind. People she had known her whole life were being driven off their land. Corporations even wealthier than the Amish themselves had moved in, offered sums of money that seemed impossible to refuse, and then, when that hadn't worked, had threatened them.

Rachel was beginning to change too. I knew she had strong feelings about leaving the Amish community by then, vanishing like the others had, though she never came out and said it to me, only hinted at it. For the first time, she had begun to complain about the tediousness of her life. Once she had even tried to leave, she said. She had packed up a bag with clothes and food but had stopped when she got to the highway near her farm, realizing she had no money and did not even know which direction led to town. With each Friday our time together seemed to go by quicker, and each time it got harder for her to go back home.

I think now that she wanted me to do something. It was not unusual for Amish women to marry at fifteen or sixteen, and I know that she was under a lot of pressure that summer to get married. Sometimes I tried to imagine what my parents would say if I brought her home with me, explained to them that she would be moving in. I imagined her coming to college with me and taking classes. I would get carried away sometimes, ignoring the absurdity of it, wanting to believe it could work.

It was a good summer for Tanner and me, our best, I think. Though we did very little until Friday nights. Days we stayed inside because of the heat and watched horror movies and drank iced tea by the gallon and nights we drove around by ourselves in Tanner's truck planning what we'd do the next Friday. We were wasting time, wasting our lives our parents said, and it felt good. That next year would be our last in high school and I think we were aware, even then, that we were nearing a pinnacle of sorts: the last summer we would still be young enough to collect allowance and get away without working jobs.

Our parents were never home that summer. There were cocktail parties and barbecues five or six times a week on our street and it seemed that almost every night the parents in the neighborhood got trashed, never stumbling home before one or two in the morning. Sometimes Tanner and I would show up at a party just to steal beer. We would stick ten or twelve cans into a duffle bag and then go back to my house and drink them on the back porch, and sometimes end up falling asleep in the backyard by accident.

In late July we started driving the truck out into the deep country during the days. The roads were all dirt out there and illegal to drive on. Occasionally we'd go out on a Saturday afternoon, hoping maybe to see Rachel or one of the girls Tanner had met the night before.

It was different out there. Aside from the humidity and the bugs, it was somehow depressing to watch all the young Amish kids working in the fields in such heat, fully dressed in their black wool suits, struggling with their ancient and inefficient tools, horse-drawn plows, steel-wheeled wagons. It seemed cruel.

One Friday night I borrowed Tanner's truck and took Rachel to the other side of town to see my house. We parked outside, just looking at it, not even talking. That night my parents were having a party and inside we could hear people laughing and the record player going. I could imagine my father slumped in his big leather recliner, surrounded by a circle of drunk guests, telling stories, and my mother carrying around trays of pierced olives and glasses of cold gin. Later on I knew my father would step outside and begin wrestling people, and everyone would yell "Go Coach! Pin 'em!" My father had been a wrestling star in college and whenever he drank, he'd start challenging his guests.

The thought of my father rolling around on the lawn with another grown man depressed me and I suddenly wanted to go back to the diner. But Rachel seemed happy listening to the music and laughter from inside.

After a few minutes she said, "Let's go inside."

I looked at her then and suddenly thought of what my father would do if I brought my Amish girlfriend into his house while he was throwing a party. My father, like most, did not like the Amish.

"Let's go," she said. "I want to try a beer."

I told her that it would be easier if I went inside and snuck the beer out to the truck myself.

A few minutes later I emerged with a couple of six packs and we drove down to the river and drank all twelve beers. Afterwards we lay down in a patch of grass near the water and acted silly. We felt loose and were affectionate with each other. It was Rachel's first time being drunk and she was being funny about it, kissing me in strange places: my elbow, my eyelid, my pinky.

Then at one point—I can't remember exactly—I started to understand that she was trying to tell me something: that it was okay. We could. That is, she would, if I wanted to. She was gripping my body tightly then, and it surprised me. And it scared me, too—because it did not feel tender anymore, but angry almost—and I know now that whatever she was trying to do, whatever she wanted that night, did not have anything to do with me.

And even though we never did, she still cried for a long time afterward, and I held her. And later, when I drove her back to the diner and we said good night, I was scared that I would never see her again.

In late August Tanner and I drove out into the deep country for the last time. Rachel had not showed up at the diner for two weeks and I had hopes of seeing her. I needed to talk to her. And Tanner, my best friend, drove me around all day.

We never did see her. Though we did see Isaac King as we were driving out toward the highway. It surprised us to see him and we stopped for a while and watched him working in the field. He was the equivalent of a foreman, in charge of the younger boys, probably his brothers and cousins. It was strange to watch him at work. He was a different person out in the fields, not quiet like he was at the diner, but loud, animated. He moved around the fields swiftly, like an animal, and the young boys listened to him and even seemed a little scared of him.

We parked up on a hill, out of sight. We were still scared of him ourselves, even from a distance. I can tell you now that I did not really hate him. But those nights I had watched him take on four or five kids at once, I believed that I hated him. I hated him for never acknowledging the futility of the situation, for not bowing his head like the others and going home. For not accepting his place like the rest of us—like my parents did, like Tanner did, and like I did.

He must have spotted us before, because he came up slowly from behind the truck and surprised us. He might have thought we were two of the kids from the diner who beat him up every week, looking for some more action. But if he did, he didn't say anything. It was illegal for us to be on that land, even illegal to be driving around in a car on those roads, but he never asked us to leave. He just stared at us until he realized we were not there to fight him and then he turned around and went back to the field.

Rachel finally showed up at the diner the last Friday in August. She was shy with me and distant. She told me that a lot of families in the community, including hers, were moving to Indiana at the end of November, after the harvest. The town was growing quickly, she said. It was just a matter of time before they would be forced to leave. She looked at me very solemnly as she said this.

"So what does that mean?" I said. "You're leaving for good?"

She nodded. "I think so."

I took her hand. "That's terrible," I said.

"I know," she said. "I know."

I've sometimes wondered what would have happened had I asked her that night to leave her community—to marry me and come live with me and my family. I thought of asking her even then, but it would have been a cruel thing even to suggest. My parents would have never agreed. It was an absurd thought, when you got right down to it. I was a pretty good student, after all, college bound.

Rachel had been begging me to take her to a movie all summer. She had never seen one before. So instead of spending our last night talking as we usually did, I took her to a rerun of an old Boris Karloff film playing at a place called the Skinny-Mini.

After the movie we drove around for a long time, just talking, though neither of us ever brought up that last night we had been together. I am certain now that she had been thinking about something else as we had watched the movie, and then later as we drove around. And somehow I could tell, even before she said the words, that she wasn't going to miss it.

We drove through town without talking. Rachel seemed disinterested, not even looking out the window. And the town seemed sad now, in the way every town looks sad right at the end of summer. It seemed cold already and empty, as if all the possibility Rachel had seen in it that summer had disappeared and now it contained only the same dismal potential it had every year.

It's strange, but I was not angry at her for leaving like this. I could tell she was not happy about it. And as we drove back to the diner I suddenly wanted to tell her how much I had enjoyed the time we had spent together, how much it had meant to me. I wanted to assure her that I would not forget her. But I never did.

When we got back to the diner, there was a crowd in the back lot, as usual. We walked over and saw Tanner watching. He was alone.

"Ten minutes," he said. "Fucking unbelievable."

Isaac King had been up for ten minutes. It was a record.

Kids were gathered around the circle, shouting, jockeying for position. I moved in closer to the group and found a spot near the edge. I could see that Isaac King was still up on his feet, his arms flailing.

What I never understood was why he never gave up. It shows that he was not right. Because even if he had been able to do the impossible—defeat five at once—there would be five more waiting on the sidelines. And then five more after that. And so on.

But that night it was clear that something was different. He wasn't going to let himself go down. In fact, he lasted a record twenty minutes. In the end, it took six or seven guys to finally get him off his feet and even after he'd been pinned down on his back he was still trying to move his arms and legs. Someone finally used a two-by-four to knock him out. It was an unnecessarily hard blow and even today I do not know which one of the kids delivered it. His head split open near the hair line. And when the blood started, everyone scattered.

I walked over to Tanner. "Hey," I said. "What the fuck just happened?"

"I don't know," he said. "I have no fucking idea."

It took a half hour to get him across the street and into a buggy. He was losing a lot of blood by then and had passed out. I suggested calling an ambulance, but Rachel said they never used the hospital. I tried to insist but she was stubborn about it.

"No," she said. "They wouldn't like it."

"Who's they?" I said.

But she turned away.

I never got a chance to say goodbye to her. When she left she was crying, though I knew it was not because she would never see me again.

Tanner and I went home after that and never went back to that part of town or talked about that night again. Instead we went into our senior year of high school and took the SATs, and then off to college like everyone else. I never saw Rachel again. But a few months later I found out from Tanner that Isaac King had died of a brain clot six weeks after that night. It was a small article in the paper and no allegations were made.

These days almost all of the Amish have left. Most have sold their land off cheap to real estate agencies and contractors and gone west to Indiana and Iowa. We have new malls and outlet stores where their farms were, and out where Rachel used to live, actors dressed in Amish costumes and fake beards stand along the thruway, chewing on corncob pipes and beckoning carloads of tourists to have their picture taken with them.

I am twenty-nine years old now and not married. I am not yet old but some days I am aware of it closing in on me. Tanner lives in California now with a woman who will one day be his wife. But I can remember when he still lived in Leola, just a few blocks away. And when I think about Rachel now, I think mostly about those races we used to have out across the railroad bridge, thirty feet above the water, and I still shudder at our carelessness, our blind motions, not watching where we were stepping, not even considering what was below us.

merkin

LAST WEEK LYNN CALLED ME AT WORK to remind me of our dinner date. I was sitting in the rec room at the Center preparing my lesson on creative memories for the class I teach and a few of the kids beside me were shifting in their seats, going over their new editions of *Moby Dick*. I looked at them and smiled and then explained that I'd be back in a minute. This is an important call, I signed.

The children nodded solemnly and went back to their books.

Lynn seemed nervous on the phone, explaining that this time would be a little different because her father would be bringing a date—a *date*, she said softly, like it was a secret—and then she went over the usual: what I should wear, what I should say, what types of new developments there had been in our relationship.

For the past three years I have been pretending to be Lynn's boyfriend whenever her father comes to town. I do this for Lynn because she asks me to and because I know it means a lot to her. Her father is nearing eighty and already mostly gone on the medications that he takes, and it doesn't make a difference that I'm fifteen years younger than her. All that matters is that I'm a man.

This year, as I said, Lynn's father was bringing a date and Lynn explained to me that this woman he was bringing must be serious if he was willing to introduce her, though she also added that her father didn't want us to acknowledge that she was his girlfriend. "He's referring to her as his 'friend,'" she said, "so that's what we have to call her too."

"Okay," I said.

Then she launched into a long list of things I needed to remember: the new car she just bought, her income tax fine, the settlement on her house.

In the distance I could see the children huddled over their books, silently mouthing the words to themselves.

Most of the children I teach have a progressive bilateral hearing loss, meaning they were born with perfect hearing or maybe only a unilateral hearing loss, but have gradually gone deaf over the years. In some ways this makes them harder to teach than the kids who were born deaf, those who never had that fleeting hope that their hearing loss might one day recover. But when I see them like this, working so hard to mouth out each word that they read, I wonder what it is that keeps them going.

"There are other things too," Lynn said when she finished, "that I'm forgetting."

"You can tell me when I get home," I said. Lynn lives across the street from me, though she often forgets this.

"Were you even listening to me?" she said.

"Of course I was."

She sighed, and I could hear someone screaming in the background.

"Look," I said. "It's going to be fine, honey, okay? It's going to be just great."

The neighborhood where Lynn and I live is located in a part of Houston called the Heights. Quiet residential streets in a mostly middle class area. None of the people in our neighborhood are rich, but most have white-collar jobs and kids and enough time and money to take care of their property. For a while the Heights was a kind of sketchy part of town, filled with your occasional crack house or abandoned building, but in the past few years it's been on the rise and lately I've noticed the cars on our street getting nicer and some of our neighbors adding on wings or, in a few cases, swimming pools.

Lynn's house is by far the nicest on the street, though modestly sized. She has a row of jacaranda trees that blossom in the spring and an oval-shaped perennial garden that lines her porch. Last year, she and her daughter Georgia tore out all of the grass in their yard and planted this new Bermuda grass, I guess it's the nicest you can get, and you can really tell the difference. Some of her neighbors have even followed suit, walking by her lawn late at night and asking her how she got her grass to look so green.

It's strange, but before I even knew Lynn and Georgia, I used to watch them, watch them as they walked around their yard, weeding on the weekends or planting flowers in the spring, washing their cars in the evening hours after Georgia came home from school. And sometimes on Friday nights I'd see Lynn out on her front porch with a stranger—sometimes a man, sometimes a woman—drinking beer and laughing. I often wonder if she ever knew that I was out there, watching her, if she even realized how much comfort it gave me just to know that she was there.

Tonight when I get home from the Center there's a message from Lynn on my machine telling me I should come over as soon as I can to go over a few of the things she forgot to tell me on the phone. Her voice sounds nervous and strained, and I hear a lot of commotion in the background.

I know that this invitation is just an excuse. In the past few months things have been bad between her and her girlfriend Delphine and I know that she likes to have me over there because it cuts the tension in the room, makes it harder for them to fight.

Delphine is closer in age to me than Lynn, but when I'm over at the house I always get the sense she's older: a parent who has been assigned to keep the house in order. To keep us from drinking too much, or forgetting to mow the lawn. Delphine is fastidious to a fault, and I know that this is something that sometimes annoys Lynn, the way that Delphine will set up the table for dinner, putting out extra knives and forks that aren't even necessary, the way she irons her clothes with starch and makes sure that the air conditioning unit is never without a filter.

Delphine is not a bad person, just hard to like. Hard to get behind from my perspective. I'm not rooting against her, just not rooting for her. Whenever I'm over at the house, she throws a fit and complains about needing more space or about how I sometimes don't even knock when I arrive. Lynn thinks that she feels threatened by me, by our closeness, and so when I'm there, I try to be nice to her. I ask her about her photographs or her prints, and sometimes even ask to see them.

For the past month Delphine has been working on a show in Austin and twice a week she drives over there and spends the night with a woman she used to date. If Lynn was a person who was prone to jealousy she'd be suspicious, and have every right to be, but she's not that type of person. She simply smiles and waves her off and when I ask her later on, as we're sitting over dinner or drinks, if it bothers her that Delphine is staying with her ex-lover, Lynn will wink and say, "Honey, I'm too old to get jealous. As long as she comes home to me, I don't really care."

And the way she says it, rolling her eyes and patting my hand, I believe her.

That night, when I arrive at Lynn's house, I find the front door open and the downstairs dark. I make my way down the hallway and call out her name. "Hey, honey," I say, when she doesn't respond. "I'm home."

In the days before her father arrives we sometimes play a game in which we practice terms of endearment on each other, but tonight I can tell she's not in the mood.

She's in there, she mouths to me, when I arrive in the kitchen, then motions toward Delphine's darkroom.

Oh, I mouth back. *Sorry*.

In the other room, the room that used to be Lynn's study but now belongs to Delphine and Delphine's photography equipment, I can hear Delphine putting on a tape of some type of European punk band.

"I have a headache!" Lynn yells to Delphine through the door and a moment later the music goes off.

"What's with you tonight?" I say.

"I don't know," she says. "Nothing. Everything." She looks at me and shrugs. "Georgia's mad at me."

"Oh yeah?" I say. "And why is that?"

She looks over at the hallway where Georgia's bedroom is, then whispers, "I caught her surfing on the internet again."

"Oh."

Lynn has become paranoid about the internet, all the horror stories you hear about cyberstalkers and weirdos. She only allows Georgia to use it for school or to e-mail her father.

"She said she hated me," she says.

"Really?"

"When I unplugged her computer."

"Well," I say, taking her hand. "She's just a kid, you know."

"I know," she says. "But she's never said that before."

I look at her. "Maybe I should go," I say.

"No," she says. "I want you to stay." And then she reaches down and grabs a bottle of wine she's hidden beneath her chair. "I'm in the mood to get drunk."

Lynn is a talented cook, and in the five minutes it takes me to uncork the wine and pour us each a glass, she has heated up a dish of pasta primavera and doled out two generous servings onto plates. Georgia is in the other room pretending to study, but more likely talking with her friends, and Delphine is still in her darkroom mixing up some chemicals. Lynn is wearing an apron and has her hair pulled back and looks at once exhausted and sublime.

"I have an idea," she says to me later that night after we've worked our way through most of the wine and Georgia has gone to bed.

"Okay," I say. "Let's hear it."

"I was thinking that maybe we could tell him we're going to Europe this year."

"Europe," I say. "Why Europe?"

"I don't know," she says. "I've just always wanted to go."

I look at her and smile. "And how are we going to pay for this trip?"

"With the money from your new promotion. Remember?"

"Oh right," I smile. "I almost forgot."

I sometimes think that Lynn enjoys creating our fictional lives more than she lets on. She always acts like these dinners with her father are some type of onerous duty she has to perform, but I never see her so excited as she is during those last few days before he arrives.

In truth, I don't think her father really notices. He's far more interested in talking about his own life or in telling Lynn what she has to do to improve hers. He's a Texas Democrat, a Texacrat, as they say, a man who's convinced that Lyndon B. Johnson was the greatest president this country ever had.

Over dinner, Lynn gives me a rundown of all the things she's told her father we've done in the past year: gone to Louisiana on vacation, sold a car and bought another, adopted a cat from our neighbor, and refinanced our house. These are all things that Lynn has actually done and so they're not that hard to remember, but before I leave she insists that I go through them one more time just so she's sure we're on the same page.

When she finishes, she takes my hand and leads me out to the porch. I can tell that she's nervous, and as we sit down on the steps beside her house, she pulls me aside in a conspiratorial way and tells me that she's thinking about breaking up with Delphine.

"When did you decide this?" I ask.

"I don't know," she says. "Probably about a week ago."

"Really?"

She nods. "It's not fun anymore," she says, "and besides I think Georgia hates her."

I nod.

"We had another fight today," she says.

"Oh yeah?"

"She accused me of being in love with you."

"That's ridiculous."

"I know," she says. "She says she senses something between us. A connection."

"Well, maybe it's just this week, you know, with your father coming."

"Maybe," she says and looks out at the yard. "I don't know."

In the distance I can see a boy on his bicycle weaving aimlessly in the middle of the road.

"So when were you planning to tell her?"

"I don't know," she says. "I was thinking maybe tonight. I don't know when I'll have the courage again."

I take her hand. "Well, I'll be up later if you want to talk."

"Okay," she says and then kisses me on the cheek.

"Good night, darling," she says.

"Good night, hon."

On Tuesdays I take the deaf children to the Java House, a local coffee house in town, and host an open mike where they read their poetry to the crowd. We always get a pretty good turnout—never more than fifty, but still a pretty good crowd—and the children always love it. They bring their parents and their friends and they stand there at the small makeshift podium that I made for them last year and read their verse.

Some of them are shy and in the moments before they go on they come over to me and sign that they're nervous, and I just pat them on the back and tell them that's fine. You can do it next time, I sign, and they will smile or nod and later when I look up I'll see them looking at me and I'll wonder if I did the right thing.

Only one of the children, José, struggles at the readings. He's a second-generation Dominican who's almost six foot three and a good fifty pounds overweight. He towers over the rest of the children, like a midwestern linebacker, hunching in the back row, waiting for his turn. No one has the courage or the heart to dissuade him, to tell him that the words he mouths are indecipherable to the hearing crowd, that the sweet beauty of his poems is somehow lost, muddled, when he reads them. Several of the other students have offered to read his poems for him, always discretely, always politely, making sure he's not around when they ask.

"No," I tell them. "I think he likes to do it, you know. I think it's important to him."

And they will nod or smile, though I know that it pains them to see, that it's disheartening to the group that the best poet among them is the only one who can't be heard.

The last time José read he had a panic attack on stage. Lynn was there that night and I could tell it upset her. We were sitting in the back row, watching, and all of a sudden José just froze up there and nobody knew what to do. We all just sat there, hoping he'd recover, but he didn't move and he didn't run off stage either. He just stood there, as if he was expecting someone to come up and help him. After a while, Lynn turned to me and told me to do something, so I went up on stage and led him off, and the audience just sat there, staring at us, not knowing whether to clap or not. Eventually another kid walked up and took the mike and everything went back to normal and I spent the rest of the night comforting José at the back of the room, telling him that it was fine, that no one had even noticed.

By the end of the night he seemed to have recovered, but I could tell it affected Lynn.

"I hate to see stuff like that," she said to me, and I could see from her eyes that she'd been crying.

"It's fine now," I said. "Look. He's smiling."

But Lynn didn't look. She just stood there.

"I think I'm ready to go," she finally said.

There's something about the children that bothers Lynn. I haven't been able to put my finger on it, but there's something about their deafness, I think, that bothers her, frightens her. Sometimes she comes to the readings and sits politely in the back, but she never cracks a smile or claps her hands. She just sits there soberly, and after it's over, she goes home. She doesn't understand how I can do it, she once told me, how I can force myself to be around such sadness every day. "Doesn't it depress you?" she asked me once.

"No," I said. "It's just the opposite. It makes me happy."

And she just looked at me and smiled, though I could tell, even then, she didn't get it.

The next day, when I get home from the Center, I see Lynn and Delphine walking to Delphine's car and I can tell right away that Lynn has chickened out. Delphine is smiling and Lynn is smiling back and both of them are holding hands as they walk toward the car.

"See you tomorrow!" Lynn yells, as Delphine pulls away, and Delphine blows her a kiss.

I feel a sadness in my gut and wonder why.

Lynn never met my ex-girlfriend Lauren, though there was a month before Lynn moved in across the street when Lauren was still living with me. We had been together for five years, most of my twenties, and when she finally moved out I felt like a part of my life had left, like I'd somehow lost all of those years, squandered them away for nothing.

Lauren was a writer and a pretty good one at that. She was a student in the graduate program at U of H, but somewhere along the way, about halfway through her MFA, she lost track of what she was doing or maybe just got bored with it, and it was during this time that she began to sleep with one of the professors in her program, a famous novelist whose name I will omit in the interest of privacy, but it was a pretty big deal all in all, something that his wife and I both eventually found out about. It was like a cold hard punch that kept hitting me in my gut day after day for almost a year, and though we eventually tried to work things out, Lauren moved out that spring and I guess that was around the time that Lynn moved in.

For those first few months that Lynn was living there, she'd look across the street and wave to me if she saw me sitting on the porch or cutting my lawn, and over time she began to come over to ask me for a smoke or sometimes a beer and it was because of this, I guess, that I began to get my life back together.

It was also around this time that she began to try to set me up with some of the women at her school. All high school teachers and all somewhat younger than me. Recent college graduates who had decided to commit themselves for a year or two to teaching before they finally met a man, or went back to school, or decided to pursue a career in something else.

What I couldn't explain to Lynn, and still can't, is that the thought of being with any of these women, someone other than Lauren, was impossible for me to imagine. I couldn't imagine sitting with them at night or lying with them in bed. I couldn't even imagine what I would say to them if we actually went on a date.

"Just be yourself," Lynn would say, trying to coax me on.

But in the same moment she'd be saying something like this, she'd start worrying about me leaving, about me meeting someone else and moving away, maybe back to California, where I'd grown up, or back to Boston, where I'd gone to college.

"I keep thinking you're going to leave," she'd say. "Will you promise me you won't?"

"I promise," I'd say.

"Good. Because I don't know what we'd do without you. It would break Georgia's heart, you know, and it would break mine."

"Well, we can't have that happening," I'd say, "can we?"

After I see Delphine's truck pull out of the driveway, I walk across the street and knock on the door. Lynn opens up and shakes her head.

"I know," she says. "I'm a coward. We don't even have to talk about it."

"What happened?'

"I couldn't do it. I just looked at her last night, as we were lying in bed, and she looked so peaceful and happy and I just couldn't do it."

I shake my head and laugh.

"Do you think I'm weak?"

"No," I say. "I think you have a conscience."

"I figured I'd wait until her show was over. She's been working so hard on it, you know, and I just didn't want to ruin it."

"That seems fair."

She smiles and then she pulls me inside and leads me to the kitchen.

"Will you open up the wine?" she says, turning her back to me. "I got us a special vintage tonight."

For the past three years Lynn and I have been having a little contest to see who can find the cheapest brand of wine that's still drinkable. Wine in a box is our staple and when that's not available we go for some of the cheaper American ones, the ones with the fake modern art on the label or the picture of the vintner holding a rake. Once in a while we'll splurge for a Bordeaux or a pinot noir, but for the most part we stick to those wines without discernible vintages or years. Wines called simply "red" or "white," or one time "pink."

Tonight Lynn pulls out a brand with a picture of a cartoon frog on the label and laughs. The wine is called Señor Frog.

"Drink at your own risk," she says, pulling out a mason jar and filling it to the lip. Then she slides it across the table and winks. "$2.99 on special."

"Wow," I say. "You've outdone yourself, haven't you?" Then I put the jar to my lips and take a sip. "Delicious," I say.

"Liar," she smiles.

On nights like this, when Lynn is a little off-kilter, she often tells me things about her life, things that she would normally avoid. She talks about her early years in New York or those months just after her husband left when she realized she was bi. But tonight I can tell she's not in the mood, and as we work our way through most of the bottle of wine, I can see her growing melancholy and tense. I figure that she's thinking about Delphine or Georgia, but when I finally ask her what's the matter she just looks at me and shrugs.

"I don't even know her name," she says after a moment.

"Who?"

"His friend," she says. "That woman he's bringing. I don't even know her name."

"Well, maybe he's just nervous about it," I say.

"I don't know," she says. "Maybe." Then she looks out at the yard, and I catch her wincing. She sighs. "You know," she says after a moment, "his first was when I was nine."

"His first?"

"His first affair. It was with this woman who used to live across the street from us. This woman named Mrs. Ross. I went to school with her sons."

I look at her. "Did your mother know?"

"I don't know," she says. "I think she probably did. He never went out of his way to hide it from her and she never went out of her way to confront him about it. I used to hate her for that, you know, for not confronting him."

I look at her and nod. Then I reach for the wine and pour her another glass.

"I think I've probably had enough of this," she says after a moment, pushing back the wine. "Who would have thought it would be such a depressing vintage?"

"I know," I say. "Señor Downer, right?"

"That's right," she says, and laughs.

Before I leave Lynn invites me to sleep on the couch, but I decline. "Only if it would make you feel better," I say.

"It would," she says and then she kisses me on the cheek. "But that's okay." And then she shows me to the door and gives me a hug. "So I was thinking Mexican tomorrow. Daddy loves Mexican, you know."

"Okay," I say. "That sounds good."

"Unless he wants to eat at his hotel, which he probably does."

"Whatever you want," I say. "Just let me know."

Then Lynn walks over and puts her arm around me. "You know what you are?" she says after a moment, pulling me toward her. "You're my beard."

"I thought only gay men had beards."

"No," she says. "Lesbians have beards too."

"Shouldn't it be called something else?" I say.

"Like what?"

"I don't know," I say, trying to think of a female equivalent, something that won't offend her.

"I think it's called a merkin," she says finally. "I heard that once. The male equivalent of a beard."

Then she leans over and kisses me, this time on the lips, a drunk, meaningless kiss.

"I think I should go," I say after a moment.

"Okay," she says, and lets me.

The next day when I go into work I find José sitting by himself in the small Japanese garden outside the Center. He is smoking a cigarette, which some of the teachers allow him to do. It's against the school's policy and they don't openly condone it, but when he takes a second to step outside they usually turn the other way. It's the general consensus that smoking is the least of José's troubles.

Are you excited for the reading? I sign to him.

He nods and smiles. Then he pulls out a piece of paper from his pocket.

This is what you plan to read?

He nods, then hands it to me. The poem is long and almost illegible, but I'm able to make out the first few lines:

I am the absence of a person / a mouth without a voice

I pretend to read the rest, though it's hard to make out, then give him the thumbs up.

Beautiful, I sign.

"Thank you," he says.

In addition to being deaf, José has diabetes and suffers from severe depression. They think he might be bipolar and have started medicating him accordingly. He seems to have gotten the bum end of almost every family gene, and yet you'd never know it from the way he acts. Both of his sisters are lean and handsome, scholarship students at Rice. They come to his readings sometimes and sit in the back, but otherwise stay hidden in their dorms. *They're too busy studying,* José will explain to me when I ask. Or: *They have boyfriends, you know.*

Last year José's father, who works for a company that specializes in life-size vintage video game consoles, donated one of the original Galaga machines to the Center.

The children loved the game, of course, and you could tell that José himself took some pride in the fact his father had donated it. For a whole week afterward he walked around the school with a big smile on his face, and it made me happy to see him this way, though it also made me sad to think that this was the only time his father had ever shown his face at school.

When I leave the Center later that day José is still sitting on his bench beside the garden. He is going over his poem, mouthing the words quietly to himself.

I walk over and stand before him and after a moment he realizes I'm there and looks up.

I wanted to wish you good luck, I sign.

You're not coming?

I'm going to try to come later, I sign, but I might miss the beginning.

I'm going last, José signs.

I know.

He nods.

Are you okay?

Yes. Why?

You look sad, I sign.

He pauses for a moment before he looks at me and smiles. "Yeah," he says. "So do you."

A few weeks after Lauren left me she sent me a long letter in which she cataloged in detail everything that had gone wrong in our relationship, starting with her initial infidelity with her professor and ending with what she called our "communication breakdown." She accused me of being distant and self-involved. She claimed that I never made an effort to listen to her, that for me it was simply a matter of being together, that we didn't have to actually talk. She claimed that I wasn't giving her what she needed, that I was too content with the status quo. She wanted me to be more assertive, she said, less passive. She wanted me to want things, just like she did, and she wanted me to see a future for us.

You're a twenty-six-year-old guy who likes to smoke pot and play video games, she wrote me at the end. *This isn't what I bargained for.* Then she signed it *Love, Lauren* and wrote a little postscript telling me not to contact her.

I did contact her, however, a few weeks later. It was late at night and I was stoned and I ended up writing a point-by-point counter-argument to her letter, explaining how each one of her claims was weak and unfounded, how she was using my past behavior to justify her actions. *I don't like being reduced to a type,* I wrote at the end, referencing her comment about the pot and the video games, and then I signed it *Love, Michael.*

As soon as I sent it off, I regretted it, and when I read it over the next day I felt depressed. It was filled with non sequiturs and faulty logic, not to mention spelling errors and typos. I had written it in a heightened state of conviction, but now, as I reread it, it seemed simply juvenile, defensive. I thought of writing her another e-mail, apologizing and explaining that I had been stoned when I wrote the first one, but I figured that would only confirm her convictions about me.

Instead, I just deleted it and waited for her reply. But her reply never came.

Sometimes I think it would be better if I was more like Lynn. But when Lynn's husband cheated on her, she made no attempt to seek revenge or demand retribution from him. She simply went on with her everyday life and then, after a lot of counseling and conversations, asked him for a divorce. It was broke, she told me later, too broke to fix. But when I asked her why she wasn't angry, she simply smiled and said, "It takes two people to break a marriage, honey. And I was one of those two people."

When I arrive at the hotel desk, the concierge informs me that the guest staying in room 412 has departed for the evening, but that a note has been left for me. I take the note and open it. In big bold letters Lynn has written: "DINNER HAS BEEN CANCELLED," then in smaller letters beneath: "Come meet me at the bar."

I ask the concierge where the bar is and he points me toward a hallway near the elevators.

At the back of the dim lit bar, which is decorated like an exotic tiki lounge, I find Lynn sitting at a small glass table all alone, drinking a daiquiri out of a tall glass.

"What happened?" I say.

"Dinner has been cancelled." She shrugs.

"Did you see your father?"

"Nope." She shakes her head.

"Did he leave you a note?"

"Yep."

"What did it say?"

"It said, 'Dinner has been cancelled.'"

"That's all."

"No. It also said that he was meeting some of his clients at some rib shack outside of town. Very important. He said that he hoped I'd understand and could we maybe have breakfast tomorrow morning before he leaves."

"You're kidding."

Lynn shakes her head.

"Typical," she says. "Story of my life."

"So all this preparation for nothing."

She smiles. "Have a seat," she says. "I'm getting drunk."

I sit down and wave the waitress over and order the same thing Lynn is drinking, whatever it is. The waitress, dressed like a Polynesian dancer, smiles politely and nods.

"Why don't you ask her out?" Lynn says, after the waitress has left.

"She's like twenty-two years old," I say.

"Never stopped my father," she says, and laughs.

I take her hand and smile and then we both look over at the stage at the back of the room, where a jazz trio is setting up and testing their instruments.

When the waitress returns with my drink, Lynn says, "I have something to tell you."

"Okay," I say. "Shoot."

"I think I might have just broken up with Delphine."

"When?"

"This afternoon—right before I came here."

"What happened to waiting till her show was over?"

"Delphine," she says. "Delphine is what happened."

"Do you want to talk about it?"

"No," she says. "Not really." She looks over at the waterfall, and for a moment seems transfixed. "She was reading my journal, I guess. I don't know how long, but she was reading it."

"So she knew."

"Yeah."

"What a little sneak," I say and Lynn laughs. Then she picks up her drink and takes a long sip.

"What did she say anyway?"

Lynn shrugs. "Oh, I don't know. The usual. I'm a liar, I'm secretly in love with you, I was never a lesbian, etcetera."

I laugh. "Well, do you feel better at least?"

"No," she says. "I feel worse."

A moment later she slides the note her father left her across the table. She has drawn a big black x through the entire thing and crossed out his name at the bottom. The note says basically what she said it said, though in slightly kinder words.

"You know," I say. "We can still go to Europe."

She smiles. "And who's paying?"

"I am," I say, reaching across the table and grabbing her hand.

She looks at me and laughs and then I fold up the note and slide it back to her.

"So what do we do now?" I say.

"Whatever you want," she says. "But I think we need to get out of here." Then she lays down some bills on the table and says that the drinks are on her tonight.

On the way out, Lynn stops by the front desk and drops off the note her father left her. She tells the concierge to please make sure he gets it. Then she looks at me and winks. "Retribution," she explains. "Ain't it sweet?"

After we leave the restaurant, I ask Lynn if she would mind stopping by the Java House and listening to the tail end of the reading. She just looks at me and nods.

"Of course," she says. "Why not."

"It's the last one," I say. "Otherwise I wouldn't care."

She smiles and looks out the window. I can tell she's thinking about something. Around us the streets of Houston are shimmering and bright: neon daiquiri bars, tattoo parlors, taquerias.

"I wish you were ten years older or I was ten years younger. Then we could get married," she says.

I smile. "You wouldn't really want that."

"How do you know?"

"Because if you did, it wouldn't really matter that I was ten years younger."

She looks at me and smiles, then turns away.

"Do you ever think about it though?" she says after a moment, looking out the window.

"It?"

"About us, you know. About you and me, about what it would be like if we ever dated."

"I'm too tame for you," I say.

"I'm being serious," she says.

"Yes," I say. "I think about it."

"Me too," she says, and nods. "I guess that's all I wanted to know." Then she looks at me and smiles and I feel a tension fill the car.

I realize at this moment that I could reach over and touch her, grab her hand, and she would squeeze it back. We could pull over on the side of the road and she would kiss me. I realize all of this, but it somehow seems wrong, and I know it's just the booze and Lynn's sudden loneliness, her fear of going back to an empty house all alone.

When we arrive at the Java House I can hear the sound of laughter and applause flooding out onto the street, mixing with the warm, humid air. Lynn asks me for a cigarette before we go inside.

"I need to call the babysitter," she says as I light her cigarette. "I told her I'd be back by nine."

"Okay," I say and light a cigarette for myself.

Lynn walks across the street to call her house and I stand beneath the palm trees on the curb and look through the window at the students as they read their poems. I can't make out what they're saying, but I can hear the occasional laughter from the crowd and the soft and steady applause. The inside of the Java House is warmly lit, welcoming, and it fills my heart with warmth.

I look over at Lynn and can see her gesticulating dramatically as she talks into the phone. I point at my watch, letting her know that it's almost over, and she waves back. A moment later she hangs up and walks over, putting her arm through mine as we stand there at the window looking in.

Inside, I can see José standing up and walking toward the podium, pushing his way awkwardly through the crowd. The other students begin to cheer and José just waves them off.

"There's José," I say to Lynn, and she nods.

"Let's go inside," she says.

"No," I say. "It won't matter."

And then I hold her, put my arm around her as we look inside.

José grabs the mike and says something into it, then stands behind the podium and pulls out his poem. I can tell by the expression on the patrons' faces that they can't really tell what he's saying, but it doesn't matter.

At that moment all I care about is standing there with Lynn, holding her close while she'll let me. And the two of us look on, watching José's lips, the sudden shifting of his brow, a boy unable to communicate with the world around him, speaking in a language no one knows.

storms

MY SISTER HAS ALWAYS HAD a certain power over me. Even when we were children and she was in and out of the hospital— even then, I made no move without her counsel. I did whatever she asked of me, said whatever she wanted me to say. And years later, it was me who she told about getting pregnant, me who covered for her when she spent a semester living with her thirty-year-old film professor, me who inevitably defended and protected her from our mother. So it only seemed natural that I was the one who answered the phone last summer when she called from Paris to say that she would be flying back to the States without her fiancé Richard. The call came around midnight, just after I had fallen asleep, but as soon as I heard her voice I knew that something was wrong. She spoke at length about her trip, but when the conversation got around to

Richard and why he would not be returning with her, she refused to say a word. She simply explained that she would be flying into Philadelphia the following evening and that she would be traveling alone. "I'm coming home *sans* Richard," she said.

The next night a light rain slowed traffic on the interstate, and when I finally pulled into the airport, I saw Amy sitting on the curb outside the baggage claim, leaning against two framed backpacks. She looked pale and tired, like she hadn't slept in several days. Her hair was up in a bandana and her face bore that glazed expression of transatlantic passengers. I waved to her, and when she spotted me she stood up and hoisted the two heavy packs into the trunk.

"I want to die," she said, as she slid into the passenger seat.

"It's nice to see you too," I said. She looked out the window.

"Do you want to talk about this?" I said, pulling away from the curb.

She shook her head.

"Are you sure?"

She nodded.

As we left the airport, I anticipated the long and silent trip back to our mother's house. Though I was certain that something had happened between her and Richard on their trip, I wasn't going to pry. With Amy, prying got you nowhere. It only made her retreat more. So I drove in silence, ignoring her, and then finally, as we were pulling onto the interstate, driving past the green farmland outside Philadelphia, heading north toward the wooded hills where our mother lives, she rolled down her window, lit a cigarette, and began to tell me the story.

She spoke calmly at first. She said that there had been a fight over in Spain. Not a bad fight, but a fight nonetheless. It was something about their hostel and who had paid, and a bunch of other bullshit. It had been building up for a few days, she said. At one point during the fight Richard had stood up, dropped his backpack on the ground, and said that he was going for a walk. They had been sitting in a train station in downtown Barcelona, waiting for the afternoon express back to Paris, and Richard had just walked off and left her by herself. Twenty minutes later the express train departed. And so, for the rest of the day, as the crowd thinned out and the sky darkened, she just sat on the bench, waiting for him. She knew that he had disappeared on purpose. He had done the exact same thing to her in Paris, left her sitting alone in a café for almost two hours. He was trying to punish her, she thought, or maybe just make her feel guilty for whatever it was she had done to upset him. But the longer he stayed away, the less she found herself wanting him to return. By evening, it was only her and a few Spanish families, huddled under the outdoor platform lights. She stuck around the station for another hour, but when Richard never showed and the last train to Gare du Nord arrived, she just decided to get on. She had both of their backpacks, Eurail passes, and all of Richard's money.

"Jesus," I said, when she'd finished the story. "Are you serious?"

Amy nodded.

"Does he even have a passport on him?"

She looked at me, then rolled down her window and lit another cigarette.

"Amy," I said. "Richard needs a passport to get out of the country."

"I'm aware of that," she said.

"How about money?" I said. "Does he have any money at all?"

She shrugged. "I don't think so."

I looked at my sister.

"I know," she said. "I know. I'm a terrible person." Her head was turned away. She was staring out the open window at the late evening sky, darkening beyond the hills.

"You know what he calls himself now?" she said.

I looked at her.

"*Rick*. Whenever we go to a party, he introduces himself as *Rick*. Can you believe that?"

I didn't say anything.

Outside the rain was picking up and as we exited the interstate, Amy rolled up her window and leaned back in her seat. "I don't want to marry someone named *Rick*," she said.

Our mother's house is a large, white colonial hidden at the end of a long private road in the wooded hills outside Philadelphia. Our father bought this house in the late sixties, and in the years since he died it has become a tradition that every summer, regardless of how busy our lives may be, Amy and I return to it for a long weekend in August. Our family has never been close, not in a traditional sense, but over time I think that we've all come to take this weekend seriously and, in our own way, look forward to it each year. That summer the visit was planned as a celebration in honor of Amy and Richard's upcoming wedding. It was going to be me, my mother, her new husband Tom, and Amy and Richard. Only now Richard was stranded somewhere in Spain, Tom was apparently in the hospital with a foot injury, and to make matters worse, there was a serious storm that had been moving up the eastern sea coast all week. All the back roads in the county were being blocked off, there were detours along the river, and further up in the wooded suburbs where our mother lives, police cars were blockading some of the side streets. As soon as Amy and I had made it back to our mother's house, we sat around the kitchen listening to the weather report; and then later, when it became clear that my mother and Tom would not be returning, we took our drinks into the living room and began to play cards.

I had thought that being home might raise Amy's spirits. I had hoped that she might take some comfort in the familiarity of her surroundings. But she had said almost nothing since our return. We played gin rummy in silence, and every time she lost a hand, she would put down her cards, sigh, then stand up and refill her drink. I was still having trouble processing what she'd done to Richard back in Spain.

To be honest, I had never really liked Richard. The first time I met him I knew the type of doctor he would be and the type of husband he would be to Amy. He was a tall, overbearing man who had a penchant for telling long, insipid stories about his experiences in medical school. And though I didn't like the idea of him join-ing our family, it bothered me that he had been abandoned in a foreign country and that no one had thought to do anything about it. I have always felt a certain sympathy for the men my sister has dated. It's as if there is a tacit understanding before we even meet, a consolatory nod to my sister's moods and temperament. She has never been an easy person to deal with, and I have never envied these men. But this was different. Richard was the man she was going to be marrying. In less than two months, they would be man and wife. And it seemed hard to imagine that either one of them would want to do anything to jeopardize that.

I tried several times to broach the subject with Amy, but every time I mentioned Richard's name, she would groan and bring up another thing he had done on the trip to annoy her. How he'd left her sunglasses at a restaurant in Bayonne. How he'd spent an entire day dragging her around Paris, looking for the grave of Victor Hugo. How he'd insisted on ordering every single meal in French. She spoke about him in the past tense and referred to their trip as if it were some type of pivotal juncture, an impasse, which they would never be able to move beyond. I said nothing. I watched my sister's face in silence, waiting for something in her expression to break. But her eyes remained stolid, focused on the cards.

When we finished our last game of gin, I helped her carry the backpacks up to her room, and the whole way up the stairs I listened as she complained about being jet-lagged and how she hadn't slept in two days, and then, as we stood outside her door, she put down her backpack and sighed.

I said, "I'm really sorry, Ame."

"Why?" she said. "It's not your fault if Richard's an asshole."

I touched her shoulder. "It's going to be fine," I said.

"No," she corrected me. "It's not."

My mother phoned around midnight. She and Tom had spent most of the day at the hospital, and now due to the storm they would be spending the night there as well. I could tell by the sound of her voice that she was distressed. She spoke for a while about Tom's injury, his surgery, and how he was now lying in post-op, sleeping. Then she asked how Amy and Richard were doing. I hadn't mentioned anything to her about Amy's phone call, and I saw no reason to mention it now. She had almost broken into tears earlier that year when Amy had threatened to call off the wedding, and I knew that she wouldn't quite be able to handle it when she learned that Amy had just abandoned Richard in Spain. I already had a vision in my mind of how the whole scene would play out: my mother crying, somebody slamming a door, the obligatory family heirloom shattering on the kitchen tile. I knew exactly how my mother was going to react, and I didn't want to be present when it happened. So I said that everyone was fine, more or less, and then asked how Tom was holding up. My mother explained that he was still in a lot of pain.

"He wishes you all were here," she said. "He keeps asking for you."

From what my mother had explained to me earlier, Tom had fractured a small bone in his foot playing mixed doubles at the country club that morning. Afterward, while he was still doped up on pain medication, he had blamed her, his partner, for not covering her side of the court and forcing him to make a reckless, last-second lunge at a stray ball. At sixty-four, Tom had over twenty senior tennis titles to his credit. He had a bookshelf full of trophies and a small plaque in the country club with a likeness of his pillowy face on it. I knew that his injury would be a major setback for him and that, in some way or another, we would all be held accountable.

I told my mother to give Tom my best, and then after we hung up I walked onto the back patio and flipped on the pool lights. It was raining hard now, the trees whipping around in the wind, the pool water spilling over onto the concrete deck. But it was a warm night, and despite the storm, there was something comforting about being back in a familiar setting. Across my mother's back lawn I could see my old school in the far distance, a cluster of large stone buildings at the edge of the woods, and beyond that the hills and the valley that led down to the river. In the years since our father had died, in the years since we'd been alone, this landscape had taken on an odd nostalgic quality for me. It seemed at times to belong to a different era, a different life. I could still remember, as a child, sitting on that lawn with Amy, waiting for our father to return from work. We would sit out there almost every night, as the sun went down at the edge of the woods and everything around us faded into darkness. We would just sit there patiently, laughing and talking, waiting for the headlights of his car at the bottom of the road, relieved when we saw them that he had made it back safely, assured in the knowledge that despite our worst fears, he was home.

After a while, I hit the pool lights and headed back inside. The house was dark now, and as I headed up the back stairs I could hear soft muffled sobs coming from Amy's room. I stood outside her door for a moment. But before I could knock, the sobbing stopped, and Amy said. "I know you're out there."

"Can I come in?" I said.

"No," she said. "You cannot."

The next morning, I stayed in bed for a long time, listening to the weather report. They were still issuing severe thunderstorm warnings, although it seemed that the eye of the storm was going to miss us now. Outside, there were large puddles forming on the lawn and a small tributary running down the edge of the driveway. I noticed that my mother's car was now parked outside the garage, but I had heard no sounds from inside the house. I lay in bed for another hour, reading, and then around ten I heard my mother and Amy talking in the kitchen. I couldn't make out what they were saying to each other, but from the elevated pitch of my mother's voice I guessed that Amy was spilling the story about Richard. A moment later I heard the back door slam and when I looked out my bedroom window, I saw Amy sliding into my mother's Saab and driving off in the rain. When I headed downstairs a few minutes later, the kitchen was empty and there was a large pile of dirty dishes in the sink. Through the patio doors I could see Tom in a wheelchair, tooling around the flagstone patio by the pool. He was decked out in his tennis whites, which were now soaked, and had a full cast up to his knee.

Like my sister, I found it hard to like Tom. For most of his life he had been headmaster at a prestigious prep school in Bryn Mawr. But some time after he met our mother, he decided to retire early and focus on the game of tennis, what he called "his true calling." Amy had been suspicious of Tom from the start. She was of the theory that he was after our mother's money. But I had tried to keep an open mind about him. And in truth, I had pretty much tolerated him up until the evening of our mother's wedding, when he had panicked at the last minute and had his attorney draft up a prenuptial agreement. The whole incident had been upsetting and also absurd since it was our mother's house Tom was moving into, her car he would be driving around in, and her membership at the country club that would allow him to amass more of his coveted tennis trophies. In fact, it was her money that had paid for the cast he was wearing on his foot at that very moment. I watched him try to negotiate the flagstone patio in the rain. When he reached the edge of the pool, I turned around and headed into the living room, then out to the side porch where I found my mother sitting by herself at a small glass table.

She lit a cigarette and regarded me absently.

"Are you okay?" I said.

She nodded, and then motioned for me to sit down at the table next to her. She slid her cigarettes across the glass surface and I took one.

"What's wrong with her?" she sighed. "Does she just hate everything?"

"No," I said. "She doesn't hate everything. I think she just hates Richard."

My mother sighed.

I reached over then and took the lighter from her hand. I lit my cigarette and for a long time we just sat there at the table, not talking. My whole life there had been moments like this between my mother and me, moments filled with silence. She has always struck me as an intrinsically sad woman, a woman who in many ways never found a way to fill the absence our father had left in her life. For two years in high school it had been just the two of us in the house, and I could still remember how she would sit with me in the kitchen while I did my homework. She would smile whenever I looked up, but I could always see in her eyes just how thoroughly unhappy she was. That was how her eyes had looked most of my childhood and it was how they looked now—a look that told me there had been more disappointment in her life than pleasure. After a while, I leaned over and touched her hand.

"It's going to be fine," I said. "They're just fighting. It's probably just nerves. They're nervous about the wedding."

"There's not going to be a wedding," she said.

"We don't know that," I said.

"You really think he'll marry her after a stunt like this?"

"I don't know," I said.

"Would you marry someone after they abandoned you in Spain?"

I shrugged. I didn't have an answer for that one.

My mother shook her head. "I can tell you right now that he won't."

Later that afternoon, when I got back from running errands in town, there was a note on the counter that my boss Ellen had called. Ellen ran the nonprofit art mag in New York that I had just started working for, and I knew that if she was calling me at home it must be something urgent. There wasn't a number written on the note, so I tried phoning the office in Manhattan several times, but there was no answer. After an hour or so with no luck, I grabbed a beer from the fridge and sat down at the kitchen table with a magazine. A few minutes later, as I was glancing through an article on Fritz Lang, the phone rang, and thinking it might be Ellen I ran to it— only it wasn't her. It was a male voice, faint and distant. There was a lot of static on the other end of the line and I could barely make out what the man was saying.

"Hello?" I said.

The phone hissed.

"Hello?"

"Hello," the voice echoed faintly.

"Richard?" I said. "Is that you?"

The connection clicked off.

I sat down at the table, wondering if it had been Richard, if he'd call back. But the phone didn't ring again and I decided not to mention it. I knew that mentioning it would only upset my mother, and I didn't want anyone feeling any worse than they already did. Amy came home a few hours later with three large bags from Ann Taylor. She went straight up to her room and locked the door until dinner.

Around seven the worst part of the storm passed over our house. I was in the kitchen when I felt the force of it moving through the room. Outside the window above the sink I could see lightning splitting the horizon, crackling at the edge of the hills, and beyond that a thick set of dark clouds silhouetted against the night sky. There was some thunder and a loud crash, then a moment later we lost our power. My mother went around the house lighting candles, Tom began making phone calls to the power company, and I took a flashlight from the hall and headed up to my room. I lay in bed, and despite my efforts to distract myself, I couldn't stop thinking about Richard, wondering if it had been him on the phone earlier that day. The more I thought about it, the more it bothered me, and the more it bothered me, the more it seemed like a good idea to call his parents. I figured that he might have tried calling them himself. They might know something of his whereabouts. They might even know of a way to get him out of the country. But that evening at dinner, when I mentioned the idea to Amy, she said that under the circumstances there was absolutely no way she was calling his parents.

"They don't even like me," she said, sipping her wine.

"Just a suggestion," I said.

Amy groaned. "No fucking way."

We were all sitting around a candlelit table in the dining room, drinking wine and eating braised chicken that Tom had somehow managed to prepare in the dark.

"No one deserves to have something like that happen to them," Tom announced from the end of the table. He had been quiet up until that point—most likely at my mother's admonition— but he was on his second glass of wine now, and I don't think he cared.

Amy pretended not to hear him and kept talking. "His parents told him he was making a mistake by marrying me," she said. "They told him he'd regret it. Can you believe that?"

"Well," Tom smiled. "Under the circumstances, I think that you've provided sufficient evidence for such a claim."

Amy made a face, then went back to eating.

Tom shook his head. He leaned back and folded his arms. At

times like this, it was easy to picture how Tom had once been a headmaster. "All I know . . ." Tom began.

"You know what, Tom?" Amy said. "I don't really care what you know."

"Amy," my mother said.

Amy dropped her fork on the table, and stood up. "Look at him, mother," she said, pointing at Tom. "A wheelchair? The man breaks his toe and he gets a fucking wheelchair."

"He's in a lot of pain," my mother said.

"It was the talus, not the toe," Tom said.

"Whatever," Amy said.

"Would you like me to produce the X-rays?" Tom said, raising his casted foot above the table, as if it was indisputable evidence.

"No," Amy said. "I'd like you to shut up."

My mother started crying then. A moment later Amy left the table and disappeared up the stairs, and Tom and I were left alone, staring at each other. Tom winked at me, as if he thought I might find some secret humor in the situation, but before he could say a word, I excused myself and went upstairs to my room to smoke. Through the wall between our bedrooms, I could hear Amy crying now. She was saying, *I hate you, I hate you*, though I couldn't tell whether she was directing the statement toward Tom or Richard.

It bothered me, in a way, that I hadn't defended her at the dinner table. I couldn't pretend to understand my sister's logic all the time, but over the years I had learned to accept her moods, her mercurial temperament and her sudden, unexpected rages. It was something that had bloomed slowly inside of her in the years since our father had died. A *difficult seed*, was what our family therapist had called it.

I sat up in bed and knocked on the wall between our rooms. Amy stopped crying, sneezed, then told me to leave her alone.

"Do you want to talk?" I said through the wall.

"No," she said. "I do not want to talk."

The rest of the evening was a practice in avoidance. Amy stayed in her room, calling her friends to complain about Richard, Tom retired to the living room to listen to the weather report on a portable radio, and my mother sat by a small candle in the kitchen reading George Elliot. I stayed in my room and listened to the storm passing over our house. Around midnight I wandered downstairs and found Tom half-asleep in front of his radio. I turned off the sound and his head jerked up. He smiled and motioned for me to sit down.

I wasn't in the mood to talk to Tom. In fact, I tried to avoid it whenever possible. But at that moment it didn't seem like I had much of a choice. So I sat down on the couch across from him, and he began to grill me on the U.S. Open, asking me who I favored to win the whole thing. He was drunk and it was hard for me to follow his train of thought. He said that if "monkey face" Sampras didn't win it all he'd be surprised. On the women's side, he favored Hingis. From time to time he would stop and reach down to tap his cast, as if to reassure himself that his foot was still there. When he finished with the U.S. Open, he began to talk about his own career, his designs to play tennis on the pro circuit, his tragic knee injury in his early thirties, and later, his reemergence as a senior champion. The story of Tom's tennis career didn't seem to be nearing any type of conclusion, so after a while I sat up and explained that, to be honest, I didn't really follow tennis. He looked at me for a moment, then frowned.

"I imagine you must play," he said.

"Not since I was a kid."

"Well, you should take it up again," he said.

I shrugged. "Maybe."

Tom frowned again. Then he rolled over to the other side of the room and began refilling his drink. "You know, I'm not happy about the way I acted tonight," he said after a moment. "I mean that. Alcohol has never brought out my best qualities. I'll be the first to admit it. But I want you to know that I love your sister. I think of her as my own daughter." He cleared his throat and looked at me. "And you as my son."

I looked down at my feet.

"I've never had children before," he continued. "I've been a teacher and a headmaster. But that's a different type of thing altogether." He seemed to be waiting for me to say something.

"You know, it's late, Tom," I said after a moment. "I should probably be heading up to bed."

Tom rolled over to the couch and parked his wheelchair beside me. I worried that he might try to lean over and hug me, but instead he just put his hand on my shoulder and smiled. "Tennis," he said. "I want you to think about that, son."

The next day at lunch there was another phone call from Richard. We were all sitting around the dining room table, picking at the pesto-turkey sandwiches Amy had prepared as a peace offering for her behavior the night before. Earlier in the morning our power had been restored and Tom had gone into the kitchen to run the dishwasher as a kind of celebration. He was the one who had answered the phone call from Richard, and when he rolled back into the room, he handed the receiver to Amy with a face. It was drizzling outside, a light summer rain, but Amy took the phone out onto the patio anyway. Tom rolled up to his spot at the table, and we resumed eating, trying not to look out the window.

"Two months," Tom said, after a long silence. "Two months before I'm back in action."

"That's not too bad," my mother said.

"Not too bad?" Tom said. "That's only the entire summer season. That's at least three tournaments I'm missing." I could tell by his tone of voice that he still blamed her for his injury.

"Aren't there fall tournaments?" I asked.

"No," he said, shaking his head. "Those tournaments are bullshit."

I looked out the window then and noticed Amy pacing back and forth by the edge of the pool, making large, dramatic gestures with her arm. I knew that whatever she was saying to Richard was not good. In a moment, she clicked off the receiver and walked back inside through the sliding-glass patio doors. She was dripping wet and I could tell by the puffiness around her eyes that she'd been crying. Nobody said a word, not until Amy sat down at the table. Then my mother, unable to restrain herself, said, "Is Richard okay, honey?"

Amy looked at her and nodded.

"Is he going to be able to leave the country?"

Amy nodded again.

"And you're sure he has enough money?"

"Jesus, mother. Don't worry about Richard."

"Well, I'm just curious."

"Well, he's fine. In fact, he's totally fucking great. The person you should be worried about—if you're really curious, Mother—the person you should be worried about is *me*." Without excusing herself, Amy stood and trudged through the kitchen, up the back stairs.

Tom shook his head. "I'm not saying anything," he said. "I'd just like to point out that I'm not saying a word."

My mother gave Tom a look, then stood up and began clearing the table. "It's just as well," she said to no one in particular. "It's not as if we could've afforded a wedding."

Tom cleared his throat, and stared at her.

"What are you talking about?" I said.

"I'm talking about your father's money."

I looked at her.

"Tom made some bad investments," she said.

"Now, hold on," Tom began, but before he could finish, my mother walked out of the room and up the back stairs. I expected Tom to roll into the hallway after her, but he didn't move. He just sat there, bewildered and scared. He wouldn't look at me.

"How much money did you blow?" I asked.

"This is between your mother and me," Tom mumbled, still looking down.

"Tom," I said. "How much?"

Tom looked out the window. Then, without saying a word, he turned around and rolled out of the room.

I spent the rest of the afternoon in my room, trying to process the slow and steady demise of our family. In the years since our father had died, it seemed that a cloud had descended upon us, a cloud the precise size and shape of our house, and that nothing in the intricate fabric of our futures would ever be the same. In the books the psychologists had given to Amy and me as children, I remembered reading stories about people who claimed that after one of their parents died they were just never happy again. I understood this to be the case with my sister and sometimes with my mother.

Life goes on, but it's different now. It's softer, duller. The highs are less high and the lows seem to have an endless depth to them, a depth you have to be wary of falling into. As I lay on my bed that afternoon, it occurred to me that Amy had probably spent most of her life on the edge of that depth, unwilling to let herself fall in, but frightened all the same by its presence. Now it seemed that she had finally given in. And that afternoon, as the phone rang off the hook, she stood in her doorway and instructed us not to answer. It was Richard, she said, and she was not talking to him.

Downstairs, I could hear Tom whining about the fact that my mother had told the entire world about his investments. He kept saying, "The market's fickle, Helen. It's too early to tell."

"I'm not talking about this here," my mother said at one point, then a few minutes later I heard the door slam and saw them both head outside to the garage. My mother helped Tom into her car and then they drove off, leaving his wheelchair in the driveway.

That night was supposed to be the big celebration in honor of Amy and Richard's engagement. My mother had ordered an elaborate meal earlier in the week, and I guess she must have forgotten to cancel it, because at seven o'clock sharp two caterers showed up at the front door and dropped off several large food trays— salmon mousse, marinated veal chops, grilled eggplant, Seckel pears poached in red wine. All this amazing food, and nobody here to eat it. I didn't have an appetite, so I left the trays in the dining room and went upstairs to knock on Amy's door.

"Dinner's here," I announced.

"Not hungry," she said through the door. I stood there for a moment, then turned the knob slightly and looked in. Amy was in her blue sweatpants and Amherst sweatshirt, smoking and paging through an old photo album. After a moment she looked up at me and smiled.

"Do you want to get drunk?" she said.

My mother has always kept a stocked bar. She and my father used to drink every night when they were younger. They drank straight Scotch and then switched over to gin and tonics in the summer. A lot of people are social drinkers, but my parents were nightly drinkers. They'd start with a drink before dinner, then keep going till it was time for bed. My mother had cut down some since she'd married Tom, but Amy and I were still able to muster up a bottle of Tanqueray and a few bottles of mixer. The rain had stopped, so we took our drinks out on the patio where it was cool. Amy said that it had been a long time since she had gotten drunk, really drunk, and that she wanted to tonight. I could tell that she was upset, maybe even a little reckless, but I kept pouring her drinks, and she kept drinking them, and pretty soon we were both laughing about all the stupid stuff we'd done as kids. The time she had made me drink mud, the time we had almost burned down the house, the time I had thrown an apple at a white-tailed wasps' nest and gotten stung seventeen times. Before long Amy was crouched over in hysterics, and I was leaning back in my chair, happy to see her in good spirits again.

"You know," she said, placing her drink down on the floor of the patio. "You're the only one who gets me, Alex. My whole life. You're the only one who understands me."

"I find that hard to believe."

"No, it's true," she said. "Not even Richard understands me. Not really. Not like you do." She looked out at the pool.

"I take it the wedding is off."

She smiled, poured more Tanqueray into her drink. "Can I tell you something?"

"Sure."

"Okay. But if you say anything, I'll have to cut off your balls."

"Okay," I said. "Understood."

She lit a cigarette and leaned back in her chair. "I didn't leave him. He left me."

"What are you talking about?"

"Richard. When we were in Spain. He said he had some reservations about marrying me. That day at the train station, he took his passport and some money and said he wanted to travel some more, by himself. He left his backpack and everything. He said we needed some time apart."

"You made the story up?"

She nodded.

"Amy."

"I know," she said. "He just called this afternoon from Madrid to say that he misses me and that he can't believe what he did. He's begging me to forgive him now. One night by himself and he panicked." She laughed. "He's getting on the first flight home tomorrow."

I leaned back in my chair. "Jesus."

"Don't tell Mom," she said. "It'll be easier if she thinks it was my fault."

"Right."

"I mean it," she said. "You can't say a word."

"You got it," I said.

She nodded, then leaned over to reach her glass.

"So what now?" I asked.

Amy shrugged and looked out at the hills. "I don't know," she said. "I'm almost thirty, Alex. Thirty years old." She paused to sip her drink. "Richard and I have been together for three years, right? Three long years. You get to know someone when you're together that long. You get accustomed to them, you know. And I'm not saying that he's perfect, because let's face it, Richard can be an asshole half the time. But last year he started putting away this money for us, you know, for when we got older, and it got to me somehow, the fact that he was already thinking that far ahead."

She sighed then and leaned over and put her head on my shoulder. "I mean, really," she said after a moment. "What's the worst thing that can happen?"

I put my arm around her then, and it felt good to have the full weight of her body against me. It had been a long time, years it seemed, since she had let me hold her. I touched her hair and ran my fingers through it, and after a while, as the wind picked up, she leaned into my chest and closed her eyes. And for a brief moment I felt myself drift back to those late summer afternoons when we had sat on that patio as children, waiting for our father to return from work. I could still remember the way Amy would smile when she saw his headlights flash at the bottom of the hill. It seemed the simplest joy in the world—those lights, his car—the knowledge that the person you loved most was on his way home.

skin

CHLOE AND I ARE LYING NAKED on the floor of our tiny studio apartment drinking iced tea. It is April, unseasonably warm, and we have the windows open and the fan going. Outside it's raining lightly, and below us on the street we can hear children splashing on the slick macadam, our Dominican neighbors laughing under puddles of blue smoke. Chloe rests the sweating glass of iced tea on the pale skin above her navel and makes me promise that I will never leave her. It is a game she likes to play, and I kiss her shoulder and promise. We are both twenty-three and recently married, and in six months from now we will move out of the barrio and into a small house in north Houston. As a gesture toward our new life, we will adopt a small black Lab, who we will name Jack, and three days later, because we love Jack so much, we will buy another—a girl puppy this time—to keep him company. We will have a large front porch and a porch swing and every night we will sit on the porch with the dogs, drinking cold Coronas, listening to Chet Baker, amazed that we live in a house that has a garage and a driveway and flowering jacaranda trees in the front yard. In a year, Chloe will get a new job at a gallery in the art district—and three days after her twenty-fourth birthday, she will come home from this job, just like every other night, and sit down at the kitchen table across from me. Her hands will be moist, her hair mussed. She will look so serious that for a moment I will think she is playing a joke on me. She will light a cigarette and close her eyes. She will hold my hand and say that she doesn't yet have words for what she needs to tell me. Later that night, she will call her mother in California and I will sit in the kitchen, smoking, listening to her cry into the phone on the other side of the house. Neither of us will sleep that night, though we will not speak much either. We will lie in the cool darkness, like strangers, and the next morning, without looking at each other, we will drive through the tail end of a hurricane to a small clinic outside of Houston, where I will sit alone in a dark room, thinking of names for the child we have just signed away.

This is what will happen. But this afternoon, lying on the soft lime carpet next to her naked body, listening to the rain and laughter, I am thinking only of Chloe's skin. My young wife's pale skin, which is cool and soft like her name. Outside on the street the music picks up and Chloe rolls over and begins again—kissing first my chest, then moving lower. I close my eyes, knowing that afterward we will fall asleep together on our small mattress, as we do every night, listening to the wind in the palm trees outside our window, believing in our thick dreams that we are capable of nothing cruel.

connecticut

THE SUMMER HE WAS RELEASED from the hospital my father moved to our family's summer cottage on Maquesett Island, off the coast of Connecticut, and for most of my childhood that is where I remember him living. He managed to reside there year round, even through the desolate winter season, among the small gray shingled houses at the far end of the beach. My sister and I grew up with our mother in eastern Connecticut, in the house she had inherited, and every few weeks we would take the ferry out to the island to visit him. These trips were often brief, never longer than a few hours, and their purpose was usually to bring my father his medications or later to make sure he had not had what my mother referred to as a "setback." My sister and I were told that our father was in a recovery period, that he was taking some time on his own to work out some things in his life. This is how our mother would explain it to us on those long trips out to the island, though even then, we both seemed to understand that it was more serious than that.

We had, in our own way, grown accustomed to his absence in our lives. By then it had been a year since my father had broken down in the middle of performing a routine surgical procedure, a year since my mother had driven him to a hospital outside of Boston, where one of his friends, a colleague from medical school, had diagnosed him as having a mental illness that had been latent most of his life. It had been a year since all of this had happened, and though his decision afterward to move out to the island to live alone had left a hole in our lives, we did not talk about that hole. I was thirteen at the time and still too young to completely understand my father's illness, but unlike my sister and mother, I somehow sensed intuitively that what had happened to his mind was permanent. My mother, even years later, would insist on referring to his condition as a "temporary setback." She would tell her friends he was just going through a difficult period at the moment, a rough patch, as if she somehow believed he would one day transform back into the same man she had married when she was twenty-two. I can understand now that my mother's excuses grew out of a deep, uncertain guilt—that she, like my sister and me, blamed herself for what had happened to him. But I also know that in her heart she did not really believe these things, that she had probably let go of any realistic hope of my father's returning long before any of us. I remember the way she would hold him on those visits, just before we left. She would hold him like she was afraid he might suddenly disappear. Afterward, on the ferry ride back to the mainland, she would not talk about it. She would just read the paper silently, my sister would listen to her Walkman, and I would find a spot somewhere on the stern of the boat and stare out across the ocean, watching the island until it disappeared on the horizon.

The house we lived in, the house my mother's father had built in the late forties, sat on a small hill at the end of a private road outside of town. Through the woods on the west side of our property, you could see the edge of the country club's golf course, and on the other side, directly across, was the road, which continued for several miles through the country and then eventually into town. About a mile down the road was Elson, the private school my sister and I had attended since we were very young. Elson was a boarding school and from an early age I had discovered that there were certain benefits that went along with living so close to it. Aside from not having to sleep in the dormitories like the other students, I'd found that if I chose my moments judiciously, several times each month I could slip off into the woods behind the soccer fields and return home early. I would follow the thick line of trees to the edge of the road, and as long as I didn't do it too regularly, no one, not even the teachers, noticed I was gone. Unlike my sister, whose photograph appeared regularly in the school newsletter, who aced all of her midterms, who scored more goals than any field-hockey player in the history of the school, I was not well known at Elson. My friends consisted of two shy Filipino girls who allowed me to sit with them during the lunch period, and among the administration and faculty I was generally regarded as a quiet but odd student, a model underachiever. In truth, I probably worked as hard as anyone else in my class, but I had difficulty when it came to focusing on lectures and processing information—as if what entered my brain was somehow misdirected along the way.

In any event, the task of returning home early from school was something I had perfected to an art. It was something I looked forward to and cherished three or four times each month. When the fifth-period bell rang, I would simply wait in the lavatory until the rest of the students had filed into their respective classrooms. Then I would sneak out the back door of the school, cross the athletic fields at a quick gait, and slip into the woods behind the stone wall that surrounded our school. From there, I would find my way home by instinct, looking for certain landmarks—the Gustavsons' red chimney, the Leverings' new tennis court—until I had made it into familiar territory. When I had finally reached the spare patch of trees at the base of our back lawn, I would wait in the shadows until I was sure my mother's car was not in the driveway. Tuesdays and Thursdays were always safe bets, as my mother liked to play bridge with her group at the country club on those days, and Fridays were often reliable too, as my mother went to volunteer at a blood clinic in town. But Mondays and Wednesdays were always a crapshoot, and I mention this only because it was on a Wednesday during the fall of my thirteenth year—the year that I want to talk about—that I came home early one day to find my mother holding the hand of our neighbor, Mrs. Bentley.

The Bentleys had been my parents' oldest friends before my father had gotten sick, and though they hadn't ignored us as other families in the neighborhood had, they had all but stopped dropping by to visit in the past year. Mrs. Bentley, in particular, seemed to have slowly drifted out of our mother's life. So it was surprising to see her holding my mother's hand, and even more surprising because the way she was holding it did not seem to be in friendship, but rather in intimacy, like I had seen my father hold my mother's hand as a child, or as I had seen couples at the country club hold hands during the debutante parties each fall. They were holding each other's hands tightly and walking happily past the perennial garden and then, as they neared the hedge, my mother touched Mrs. Bentley's shoulder, Mrs. Bentley put her arm around my mother's waist, and then the two of them embraced—like two young lovers—at the edge of our family's back patio.

I imagine it must have seemed entirely safe to have their clandestine hug out there on the back patio. After all, our property was obscured by a thick wall of spruce trees on each side, and it was rare, in any case, that someone would be lurking around in the woods at this time of day. But I wonder, now, if they even cared. I wonder if they didn't secretly hope to be caught. It was the beginning of a new era in our country—the seventies—and little that had been frowned upon before, even in the bucolic suburbs of Connecticut, was frowned upon now. But for me, at the time, it seemed the most horrid and depraved of activities, and I had to brace myself against a tree trunk, as I watched my mother hug, then hug again, the woman who had driven me to swim practice as a child, the woman who had scolded me for riding my bike across her lawn, the woman who had sat in our house during Christmas parties and, perhaps drinking a little too much wine, belted out Christmas carols in a voice four octaves too high.

I had never had anything against Mrs. Bentley before then. She had always been among the least pretentious of my parents' friends, but suddenly, in the soft gray light of that October afternoon, I thought of every horrible thing she had ever said to me, every time she had told me to keep our dog Whinney out of her yard, every time she had not been home when I stopped by her house on Halloween. She and her husband had two daughters, one who was my age and attended boarding school in Vermont, and another, two years older than Kelly, who was now off at college. As young children, we had played with their kids, and later, as they grew up, the Bentleys had come over for cocktails in the evenings, Dr. Bentley talking tennis with my father out in the backyard, while Mrs. Bentley and my mother paged through clothes catalogs in the kitchen. There had been nothing to worry about then—their friendship, like most friendships among older women, was based on common interests, idle gossip and mutual concerns about their children's academic progress or their husbands' diminishing interest in them. They were close, but they were never intimate with each other. There was never a physical element to their relationship. In fact, before now, I had never seen them hug—even in the weeks after my father's breakdown they had never once embraced each other. And it was for this reason that I understood that the hug my mother and Mrs. Bentley shared out on the back patio—the long series of passionate embraces—was not done out of commiseration. It was not the kind of gentle hug you give to someone who has just experienced a loss. It was the type of hug I would read about later that year, when our English teacher assigned us *Lady Chatterley's Lover*. It was an illicit hug. A forbidden hug. A hug of love.

You might wonder how a boy of thirteen would be able to discern such a thing. You might wonder how I was able to know that my mother and Mrs. Bentley were not just two woman comforting each other on a late autumn afternoon. To be honest, I can't be sure myself. I had certainly never held a prurient interest in my mother's sex life. And I had certainly never entertained thoughts of her with other women. The idea of it had never even surfaced in my mind before that day. She was a devoted wife and a loving mother. These things I knew. But the way she held Mrs. Bentley that day was clearly not meant for public observation. And later that afternoon, when I finally surfaced from my hiding place in the woods and came through the kitchen door, my mother made no mention of Mrs. Bentley's stopping by our house. Even when I asked her what she had done that day, she simply shrugged and said that she'd run a few errands, cleaned up the kitchen, planted a few azaleas in the perennial bed. "Nothing too interesting," she said. But when she later leaned down to kiss my forehead, I found myself jerking away and then, aware that I had hurt her, running straight out of the kitchen and up to my room.

That night, I lay in bed for several hours, feigning a sudden illness, and begging off dinner. Downstairs I could hear my mother and sister laughing in the kitchen, and as I lay there, listening to them, I thought about my father. I thought about him on his island all alone, and I thought about what he would think had he seen what I had seen. He was not a loud or aggressive man. Even before his breakdown, he had been gentle and soft-spoken, a doctor who amazed his patients with his patience and sensitivity. He was a good person and I can't imagine him getting overly excited or violent about such a thing. He was of that generation of men who simply accepted the mystery of womanhood, who made no effort to try to understand their wives, but simply accepted that there were things that women said and did that they would never understand. In this way, he might have simply shrugged the incident off, considered it one of the many things about my mother he would never understand. He might not have been in the least bit threatened by it. But to me, my mother's secret embrace with Mrs. Bentley seemed to threaten the very foundation of our family. I thought more than once about saying something to my sister, Kelly, letting her know what I had observed. But I knew that she would most likely just laugh it off, call me a sicko, then run to my mother with news of my latest perverted theory. "Guess what Steven thinks," she would squeal. "He thinks you and Mrs. Bentley are lezzies!"

In the end, I decided that the best thing to do was to keep it to myself. Maybe it would all go away. Maybe it had been just a one-time thing. Everybody has moments of weakness, I reasoned. Everyone gets confused from time to time. Maybe it was Mrs. Bentley who had seduced my mother. Maybe they had simply had too much claret.

I resigned myself to these and other theories, but in the weeks that followed, what I hoped would be a passing anxiety did not idle. In fact, I became almost acutely aware of my mother during that time. I studied her as I used to study insects when I was younger, keenly aware of any subtle movement, convinced somehow that there was a hidden mystery that would be revealed if I stared long enough. In my mother's case, however, I found little out of the ordinary. She followed the same routine she always had, and there seemed to be nothing masked beneath her gentle visage, no dark desires lurking beneath her aproned frame. She seemed simply herself, which is to say slightly preoccupied, vaguely burdened, as she'd always been, by our father's absence. In the evenings she stayed home with us, reading in the dim light of the kitchen or helping my sister with her college applications, and during the day, as far as I know, she followed the same routine she always had.

Still, when I came home each day, greeting my mother with a quick kiss, I would often linger for a moment, taking in the scent of her hair, hoping, I suppose, that I might discover something—a trace of Mrs. Bentley's perfume, a whiff of wine from a late after-noon lunch they had shared. In retrospect, the elaborate fantasies I created in my mind during that time were probably much more sordid than what actually occurred between them. I do know that they continued to see each other after that afternoon, and I do know that what occurred was not the type of socializing that went on between the other mothers on our street. But I somehow doubt that their courtship, or whatever you want to call it, escalated to the proportions I imagined in my thirteen-year-old mind. Instead, I imagine that they simply spent their afternoons as they had that day in October, walking together in the yard, holding hands and talking. It would be naive to assume that they were not cognizant of what they were doing, or that they were unaware that what they were doing was, in the eyes of their neighbors, "not right". But it is possible also that while they spent their afternoons together, they did not dwell too much on it, and that when they were apart, they tried their best to forget about it altogether.

It was during this time, or shortly after this time, that I received a letter from my headmaster informing me that I would be expected to attend a meeting with him, my mother, and three of my seventh-grade teachers. The headmaster had signed his name at the bottom of the letter and then included a little note for my mother that read: *It is very important that you attend this meeting. This situation is quite urgent.*

Each term during my midterm assessment meeting, I would sit with my mother in the corner of the headmaster's office as my teachers took turns pointing out my shortcomings to her. I had trouble grasping rudimentary mathematical principles, they would explain. I took too many leisurely walks to the water fountain during history lessons. I painted the wrong types of pictures in art class. And so on. Most of the teachers agreed that I was deficient, or "not right," in some capacity. At the end of the conference, they would suggest to my mother that I receive additional tutoring after school or that I start meeting regularly with the school counselor. The headmaster would be looking out the window the entire meeting, nodding to himself, tapping his foot lightly against the oak desk, and when the teachers had finished talking, he would turn and ask me if I understood the severity of the situation. He always referred to my poor academic record as "the situation"—as in, "The current situation seems to have developed in a less than satisfactory manner." I would nod and tell him that I did.

"Do you understand," he would add, "that if you continue to perform at this level, we will have to ask you to leave school?"

Again, I would nod. There would be a brief silence in the room. Then, one by one, I would apologize to each of my teachers and make some vague but optimistic statement about how I felt myself moving in a new direction—how I thought that the future prospects of "the situation" looked good. At this point, there would be some whispering and rumbling among the teachers and then finally they would nod in unison, which meant my mother and I were free to leave. In the end, I knew that my mother would never really make me go to see the counselor. She seemed to understand that, despite my poor grades, I worked as hard as anyone else. After the meetings, she would put her arm around me as we crossed the parking lot and tell me that none of this was my fault. "You know, Steven," she would say, "you don't have to like those people."

Later, on the ride home, I would sit next to her, staring out the window. I would be thinking of my father, sitting alone in his cottage on the island, and from time to time my mother would reach over and touch my hand, as if she somehow knew what I was thinking. "Don't worry, honey," she would say. "It's not going to happen to you."

But that evening she didn't say any of these things. Instead, she simply drove without talking, and I sat next to her, watching her face, her solemn expression, as we sped through the streets of our neighborhood. When we pulled up to the edge of our driveway, my mother stopped the car on the street, and then, after a brief pause, continued down the street to the Bentleys' house. She turned off the engine and explained that she'd be back in a minute. I watched her walk up the long walkway to the Bentleys' front porch, and as she stood there in the cold night air I sensed that she wasn't quite sure why she had come or what she had wanted. After a long pause, she finally knocked on the Bentleys' door, and when Mrs. Bentley opened it, my mother let out a loud, whimpering cry, then leaned into Mrs. Bentley and hugged her tightly. Mrs. Bentley seemed to be comforting my mother, seemed to be whispering something in her ear, but I couldn't make out what she said.

When my mother returned to the car, I could see that she'd been crying, and as we continued down the street to our house, she simply looked at me and sighed. "I want you to try and do better, Steven," she said. "I think it's important that we all try to do better." I wasn't quite sure what she meant by this, but I nodded anyway, and as we got out of the car and walked to the house, I held my mother's hand and told her that I would.

"I'll try to do better," I said. "I promise."

Only now, fifteen years later, can I say with certainty that my mother and Mrs. Bentley were lovers. But I know this only because of small clues I have picked up along the way—a love letter I once found in my mother's bureau, a photo of Mrs. Bentley wedged between the mattress and the box spring of her bed. And once, when I was in high school, a conversation I heard her having one night on the phone when she thought I was sleeping. But at that time in her life, the whole involvement seemed to have little effect on her—or at least upon her outward appearance. And it was not until the weekend of Thanksgiving, almost a month after that afternoon on the back patio, that I first realized that my mother had fallen in love with Mrs. Bentley and that Mrs. Bentley had, in turn, fallen in love with my mother.

I remember that day vividly, even now. The morning was bright and breezy, unusually warm for fall, but by late afternoon, by the time our guests—the Bentleys and the Oleanders—had arrived at the house, the light breeze had become a brisk wind, and the sky had grown overcast and gray. Kelly and her boyfriend, Chad Winters, were outside in the back yard, getting high behind the tennis shed, and I can still remember the bright ember of the joint they passed, like a bright orange firefly, flickering against the light evening sky. Downstairs, I could hear my mother laughing with Mrs. Oleander in the kitchen and Dr. Bentley and Mr. Oleander watching football in the den. There was no other sound in the house, only the rich smell of the turkey basting and the sweet scent of the pecan pies that Mrs. Oleander had brought over for dessert. Mrs. Bentley had not come—at least not yet—and when I finally descended from my room and greeted Dr. Bentley, who lay supine on the couch, he made no mention of his wife's absence. He simply smiled, raised his glass in a warm, avuncular manner, and went back to watching TV. Mr. Oleander, who had once played golf with my father every Sunday, seemed similarly disinterested in me. Without looking up from the screen, he asked me who I favored—Notre Dame or Michigan—and when I admitted that I knew little of football, he simply smiled and went back to his beer.

In the kitchen, my mother and Mrs. Oleander were preparing a corn-pudding casserole and stirring gravy respectively, while the steady pulse of *La Traviata* boomed from the radio. Mrs. Oleander smiled when she saw me, mentioned how similar I looked to my sister, then went back to chatting with my mother about the cabin in Vermont that she and her husband had just made an offer on. It was clear to me, only then, how different my mother seemed in the presence of Mrs. Oleander. Unlike Mrs. Bentley, Mrs. Oleander was entirely unremarkable. Even now, as I try to imagine her face, I see only whiteness, the absence of features beneath a dull blonde bob. Hers was a face without distinction, and she seemed to have a personality to match. Mrs. Bentley, on the other hand, was at least interesting to look at. Though no longer attractive, she possessed the remnants of a striking face—a long nose and angular chin— and carried herself with the confidence of a woman who had once turned heads. If my mother's attraction to Mrs. Bentley had at all been physical, it was probably for these reasons.

In any event, dinner that day was consumed without mention of Mrs. Bentley. Dr. Bentley spoke at length about his two daughters, both of whom had been too busy to come home for the break, but said nothing of his wife. Mrs. Bentley had become like my father, it seemed: a person whose existence was not acknowledged in the presence of others. And I suppose it was then that I first realized that something had happened between my mother and Mrs. Bentley since that afternoon in the yard.

Weeks later I would learn of the Bentleys' divorce, and weeks after that the sordid details would eventually filter down from the gossiping wives at the country club to the gossiping girls at Elson: the scandalous story of how Mrs. Bentley had moved to New York City to live with another woman. But at that time the story was known only by a few, perhaps only by the adults in the room that day, and it explained Dr. Bentley's erratic behavior—his shifting moods and frequent trips to the bathroom—and it explained also my mother's gradual descent into despondency as the night continued. Refilling her glass almost as much as Dr. Bentley, my mother grew increasingly quiet, until it seemed that she had all but left us. I sensed that her sadness had something to do with Mrs. Bentley's absence, and I know that as the meal went on, and Mr. Oleander told story after story of his college football career, my mother no longer seemed to care what anyone thought of her. At one point she stood up and walked out of the room, only to come back ten minutes later, her eyes red and puffy from crying. She was normally a skilled and gracious host, but that night she seemed as if she simply wanted everyone to leave. By the time Mrs. Oleander's pecan pies were brought out to the table, the only people still smiling were Kelly and Chad.

The pie was consumed quickly, and soon after, the Oleanders departed, feigning sudden fatigue, leaving my mother and me alone with Dr. Bentley, who sat in a state of drunken malaise at the far end of the room. Chad and Kelly had excused themselves earlier, and I could now hear them upstairs in Kelly's room, blasting the b-side to *Ziggy Stardust*.

"What the hell is that?" Dr. Bentley groaned from the end of the table.

"David Bowie," I said.

"Who?" He frowned.

"Why don't you clear some of these dishes, honey," my mother said to me. And a moment later, taking my cue, I carried what was left of Mrs. Oleander's pie out to the kitchen.

There I remained, perched at the sink, running the hot water, and trying to listen through the door as Dr. Bentley whined drunkenly to my mother about his failed marriage and lesbian wife. I heard little of their conversation, just the occasional sarcastic remark from Dr. Bentley, and the soft assurances from my mother that followed. At some point I know I heard sobbing, Dr. Bentley's sobbing, and then I heard my mother leading him to the door. "I'm sorry," Dr. Bentley kept saying. "I'm terribly sorry." And it was then that I decided to walk out to the yard.

It was dark out by then, and I could see little beyond the edge of our lawn. Our dog Whinney was lying in the cool dark shadows, chewing on one of the bones my mother had given him, and shivering slightly. Since our father had left, no one had paid much attention to Whinney. He had become a reminder of our father in his prime. The dog who had followed him everywhere, the dog who had sat by his chair in the den, the dog who had greeted him each day when he came home from work, and it seemed, at times, as if Whinney himself had changed. He no longer seemed as spirited as he had been around our father, though he remained just as obedient and stalwart as ever. But that night, when I called to him, he ignored me, and instead of seeing his wide, wobbly shape emerge from the shadows at the back of our yard, what I saw was Mrs. Bentley moving across our lawn at a quick pace.

"Is he still there?" she said in a hushed voice, walking toward me. "My husband?"

"No," I said, a little shocked. "He just left."

She nodded. "I need to talk to your mother," she said.

"She's inside," I said.

Mrs. Bentley nodded and then walked slowly into the light of the patio.

"You must think I'm crazy," she said. "Standing out here in the cold."

"I don't know," I said.

"I'm afraid I'm not myself these days," she laughed. "That's why I've come to see your mother."

"She's inside," I said again. "In the hall."

Mrs. Bentley smiled at me then, tenderly, and it seemed she wanted to say something more. But after a moment, she just patted my hand and headed inside through the patio doors, into the kitchen, then out to the hallway, where my mother, her lover, was waiting.

When the rumors finally hit our school, there were stories about the mysterious woman Mrs. Bentley had gone to live with in New York. Some people claimed that they had seen this woman in town, and over time they were able to describe her in increasingly vivid detail. She had straight dark hair, pale skin, blue eyes. She was an actress, some believed, or an artist. She lived in the East Village and made turquoise jewelry in her free time. I don't know from whose imagination this woman emerged, but I do doubt very much that she existed. I'm sure it was easier for Mrs. Bentley to make up a fictional lover, someone who was extraordinary and young, someone so different from my mother that there would be no suspicion, no thought, that the woman who had lured her away from her husband lived in the safe, bucolic suburbs of east Connecticut. It must have been easier that way. Easier for her husband, easier for my mother, and easier, of course, for her. So she left, and after that night we never saw her again. Like my father she became merely a ghost in our town, one of the many who had simply disappeared. I never saw her again, but I remember on several occasions seeing letters from an anonymous sender with a Manhattan address. The first was a week or so after that night, and the others came sporadically over the next few months. My mother always set these letters aside, or stuffed them in her purse, never opening them in front of us. And later, when I would go through her desk drawers, searching desperately for these tender epistles, I would find nothing. There were other things, too. Late-night phone calls that my mother took in her room, or other times, mysterious clicks whenever my sister and I picked up the phone. Once, in the spring of that year, my mother took the train into New York for the weekend, while my sister and I went out to the island to visit our father. My mother claimed that an old friend of hers from college was in town and that she was planning to spend the weekend with her in the city. But when she came back from that trip, she seemed sullen and removed, distant in the same way she had been when our father first got sick. And I was sure then that she had gone to see Mrs. Bentley, and that whatever intimacy they had once shared was now over.

I have never doubted my mother's love for my father, but I don't pretend to believe that she ever loved him again in the same way she had when they were young. And at the same time, I don't believe that she loved Mrs. Bentley in the same way she loved my father. It's possible that after all that time alone she simply wanted intimacy, any type of intimacy, and though I don't think that she ever pursued another woman, I do believe that she loved Mrs. Bentley dearly, and I know this only because later that night, when I came in from the back yard, I heard my mother and Mrs. Bentley talking in the hallway. My mother's voice was hushed, cautious, but Mrs. Bentley was ranting feverishly, unable to keep her voice at a reasonable pitch. Upstairs, my sister and Chad had moved on to *The Dark Side of the Moon*, and were probably groping each other in the dark, but I suppose my mother must have thought I was with them, or maybe just forgotten about me altogether, because after a while she stopped whispering, and I could hear every word she was saying echoing through the house. "You can stay," my mother was saying. "You can stay and work things out."

Mrs. Bentley was crying. "June," she said. "June, what the hell have I done?"

"You can stay," my mother said again. "It's not that bad."

"It is," she said. "It's terrible."

A few minutes later, I heard the front door open, then, a moment later, click shut. I emerged from the kitchen and found my mother on the floor, leaning against the wall in the hall.

She was in tears, and seemed unable to compose herself, even for me.

"Go upstairs, Steven," she said without looking at me.

"Mom," I said, walking toward her.

"Steven," she said.

"It's okay," I said. And I wanted to tell her then that I knew about her and Mrs. Bentley, that I had seen them together that day in the yard, and that I knew, though I didn't understand, that she loved her. I wanted to tell her these things. But at that moment my mother didn't want to hear them. She simply wanted me to leave.

"Leave Steven," she said to me.

And so I did.

When my father returned from the island several years later, there was no mention of Mrs. Bentley or Dr. Bentley or what occurred between them. My father seemed to have forgotten about all those people, all of our neighbors, long ago. It was as if they were actors in a film he had once seen and no longer cared to remember. My parents lived a somewhat solitary life from that point on, rarely going to parties, or throwing dinners, or playing golf at the country club as they had before. Now they lived a quiet life, surviving meagerly off the stocks my father had bought when he was young. The doctors believed that my father had made progress out on the island, and over the years they seemed to think that his condition had slowly improved, but to me he seemed no different than he had since his breakdown, nervous and shy, dubious of his own skills, no longer the same assured and confident father I had known as a child.

As for my mother, she quickly adapted to her new life with my father, playing Scrabble and reading books in the late-evening hours, going for walks in the mornings, and monitoring his meds. To an outside observer, it might have seemed as if my mother had become a caretaker, a nurse, and perhaps this is true, but she performed her duties without complaint and I never saw her once show regret or remorse for what had happened between them.

Still, I return to that evening a lot, the evening Mrs. Bentley left, and I remember the way my mother collected herself afterward, the way she went into the kitchen and began to wash the plates, the way she put on a smile for my sister when she returned from her room, and the way, afterward, she stood at the edge of the sink, looking out at the yard, hopefully, as if she still believed that someone might be coming for her, as if she still believed that some distant shadow might emerge from the edge of the yard and reclaim her.